10.23

Claire Baldry retired from her career as a Headteacher in 2008. She is now an established writer, blogger, comedy poet and public speaker in her home county of East Sussex. She lives in Bexhill-on-Sea with husband, Chris.

Claire has published four booklets of amusing poetry and an autobiographical novella, called South Something.

Different Genes is Claire's first full-length novel.

Claire says, "Sixty is the new forty. I feel very privileged to be able to focus on my writing, now I am retired. I enjoy creating 'older' romantic heroines and placing them at the centre of poems and stories."

Also by Claire Baldry

Poetry Booklets
Simply Bexhill
Simply Christmas
The De La Warr Date
Seaside and Sailaway

Autobiographical Novella
South Something

Different Genes

Claire Baldry

Matador
9 Priory Business Park,
Wistow Road, Kibworth Beauchamp,
Leicestershire. LE8 0RX
Tel: (+44) 116 279 2299
Fax: (+44) 116 279 2277
Email: books@troubador.co.uk
Web: www.troubador.co.uk/matador
www.clairebaldry.co.uk

ISBN 978 1788036 054

British Library Cataloguing in Publication Data.
A catalogue record for this book is available from the British Library.

Printed and bound by CPI Group (UK) Ltd, Croydon, CR0 4YY
Typeset in 11pt Bembo by Troubador Publishing Ltd, Leicester, UK

Matador is an imprint of Troubador Publishing Ltd

For Chris

With grateful thanks to all my friends and family for their encouragement with my writing. Special thanks to Danielle Steele and Hilary Cisneros Mccorry for their meticulous proof-reading of the text.

This novel is set in towns and villages in Sussex, Hertfordshire and Kent. Whilst the author's detailed knowledge of the locality has been used to provide a realistic background to the storyline, road names, businesses and buildings are often invented. All characters in this novel are fictitious.

Joan's fading body lay resting on a bed in the local hospice. Her mind was numbed with a cocktail of pain-relieving drugs. Her shoulders were propped up by an uneven mound of plastic-coated pillows. Her face was obscured by an oxygen mask. The chaplain walked towards the open door of her room and peered in. She lifted an arm to signal that she wished the clergyman to approach. Father Martin drew up a chair and sat beside her.

"Do you need something, Joan?"

She pulled the mask from her face.

"Paper."

Father Martin produced a clipboard with paper from his leather case. He placed it on her chest and put a pencil in her hand. He steadied the paper, as Joan began to write.

Dear Louise

The script was barely legible.

I think you should know....

The letter was never completed. The pencil fell from her hand, and her body gradually slumped into emptiness. Father Martin removed the clipboard and pencil from the bed and returned them to his case. He pressed the emergency button and spoke the words of a silent prayer.

ONE

A Celebration of Joan

Simon took the coast road back from Rye. He had finished wandering around the market earlier than expected, so decided to stop for a short walk in Fairlight Country Park. It had been a clear autumnal day, but, by the time he reached the park, a dense cloud had engulfed the cliff top. The air was filled with damp droplets, and the sea was barely visible. He parked by the Fairlight Tea Rooms and decided to sit inside with a pot of tea for company. When the tea was no longer warm, he wandered through the plant-filled conservatory and sheltered outside under the awning. He could just catch a glimpse of Fairlight Church and the blurred horizon beyond. He found himself observing a distant group of mourners who were drifting away from the graveyard. Simon wondered where the family would gather later for the customary tea and finger food. The grey sky and murky rain added a sombre atmosphere to their steps. He glanced down at the discarded cigarette ends surrounding his feet. He was so pleased he had finally given up.

'People had adjusted easily to the smoking ban,' he reflected. 'Nine years ago, the mourners would have been allowed inside the tea shop to smoke away their grief. Now they were banished outside in the mist.'

As if reading his thoughts, an older man in a black overcoat slipped away from the group of mourners and lit up a cigarette beside him.

"Did you know her?" asked the man.

"No," replied Simon, "I was just leaving the café and I found myself watching. You?"

"Auntie Joan was my wife's cousin. I thought I'd leave the girls to chat, while I sneaked a cigarette. They don't get to meet up very often. It takes a funeral to bring a family together. You can tell they're related, can't you? They all have the same stubby body shape. Auntie Joan looked like that too."

Simon smiled at the way the man had described the women in his family.

"I see your point. They do look similar. All except that lady on the right. She is much taller and leaner."

"That's Louise. She's adopted... different genes."

Simon suddenly felt uncomfortable. He sensed he was intruding. He pulled the car keys from his pocket, apologised to the man, and made excuses to leave. As he climbed back into his Mercedes, he began to reprimand himself. He knew he was lonely, but choosing to pass the time by watching a bereaved family was, he decided, really desperate. He must take himself in hand and do something.

The family group gradually dispersed towards their own vehicles. As Simon had predicted, they headed to a private room in a nearby hotel. The tables were laid with crisp white cloths topped by sandwiches and cakes. The hotel staff were serving tea from large metal teapots.

The sign on the door read, 'Friday 30th September 2016: A Celebration of the Life of Joan Watson'.

"I'm so sorry about your mum," said a family friend to Louise.

"Thanks, Bob. She had a good long life, and I wouldn't have wanted her to suffer any longer. Her death was a relief really. Mind you, I'm not looking forward to clearing the bungalow."

"Of course, you're an only child. There are no brothers or sisters to share the task. Will the cousins help?"

"You know, I think I'd rather get on with it on my own. When I split up with Charlie, we had to discuss every single item of furniture and decide who would have what. It was very wearing. Mum's will left everything to me. At least this time I can make all the decisions on my own."

"You're probably right. Just give me a call though, when you need anything. I'll happily drive my van from Hastings to the tip for you, if it helps."

"Thanks, Bob. I just might take you up on that offer," Louise lied. She had no intention of allowing Bob to intrude upon her grief by touching her mother's belongings.

The gathering broke up shortly before 4 pm. Kisses and hugs were exchanged, and they began to return to their cars.

"Are you sure you will be okay on your own?" asked Louise's cousin, Karen.

"I'll be fine. I stayed in the bungalow for two weeks before Mum died. My bed is still made up, and it will give me time to get my head back together. I need to be alone for a while."

"Well, as long as you're sure."

"I am."

It was a long drive back from Fairlight to Sawbridgeworth. By the time Michael and Karen reached the Dartford Crossing, the traffic was crawling in congested rush-hour lines towards the tunnel.

"I never understood why Joan decided to move to Sussex," remarked Karen. "You can't get anywhere without negotiating the M25."

"Well she seemed happy enough living there," responded Michael. "Perhaps she was enticed by the sea. Fairlight is such a beautiful village, even if it does attract the mist."

"Living in a cloud sums it up," Karen spoke her thoughts out loud, "I still can't believe that Louise has never suspected. Actually, I wish I didn't know. It feels wrong that Louise was never told."

Michael felt an uncomfortable sense of guilt that he had shared Joan's secret with a complete stranger. He decided not to tell Karen about his indiscretion.

"We must be the only ones left who know. When we die, the secret will die with us."

3

Karen and Michael's car finally escaped into the faster moving traffic of the M11. Michael pressed his foot on the accelerator and began to focus on his driving. His craving for a cigarette increased the speed of the car.

Joan's bungalow was only a mile from the hotel. Louise stopped at a mini supermarket and bought herself a bottle of wine and some supper. She was soon turning the key in the front door.

"I'm home, Mum."

Louise knew her mother wasn't there, but she found the words comforting. She put the supermarket bag down on the hallway floor and switched on the lights in every room. Suddenly, the familiar furniture looked very dated. No one would want the floral curtains and patterned carpets. Oriental coffee tables brought back from Singapore in the fifties were clumsily combined with a mixture of furnishing taste from the 1970s onwards. Louise shook her head at her mother's lack of creativity. She would box up the paperwork and a few precious items, then call in the house-clearance people. It would be for the best. She would aim to complete the task by the end of the weekend. Tiredness then began to overwhelm her. Louise turned on the TV, microwaved her supper, poured herself a glass of wine and sank into the sofa. By 9 pm she was in bed.

The hallway light cast moving shadows across Louise's body while she slept. Her eyes flickered, as an elderly lady moved towards her in the night.

"Mum?"

"It's Nana. I have paper and crayons. We will draw rainbows together."

Nana took Louise's hand and helped her to create vast coloured arcs.

"We will find a pot of gold, Lou Lou."

"Don't leave me, Nana."

"I will never leave you. I will always be at your side. I will hug and protect you."

Louise woke in a sweat. Streaks of autumn sunlight were shooting through the gaps in the curtains.

"It must be morning." She grabbed the little travel clock from the bedside cabinet.

"Half past six, I slept all night."

She climbed out of bed and wrapped herself in a dressing gown.

'Tea and activity... no... strong coffee. I will need the energy.'

Louise wandered from room to room trying to organise her thoughts.

'Good thing Charlie isn't with me. He would want to sell everything.'

Coffee in hand, she sat down in front of her mother's desk. The papers were neatly organised into four, labelled, pocket files. 'Finance', 'House', 'Medical' and 'Louise'. Sorting out her affairs had been a top priority for Joan once the cancer had been diagnosed. Louise stroked the folders in gratitude. She slipped the 'House' and 'Finance' folders into a canvas shopping bag. The other two folders were placed in the bottom of a box. They could wait until later.

She began to remove her paintings from the walls and lean them against the sofa. She would need more boxes... and bubble wrap.

"You didn't think of that, did you, Mum?"

By 10 am Louise had dressed, climbed into her car, and purchased boxes and bubble wrap from an out-of-town warehouse. On her return journey, she stopped at the small tea shop next to the Country Park for another coffee and a bacon roll. She could see the distant churchyard where they had gathered the day before. Tears began to rise in the backs of her eyes.

Her mobile phone rang.

"Gillian, how lovely to hear from you. No, I'm staying at Mum's, trying to clear up her things. I'll be back at the studio tomorrow evening."

Louise blinked away her watery eyes and spoke quietly, so as not to disturb the other coffee drinkers.

"It's not too bad really. She left things pretty well organised.

I'm going to get the clearance people in next week. There's not much demand for floral curtains these days. Maybe I can phone you when I get back home?"

"Please do," replied Gillian. "You are welcome to come to Brighton for a few days."

"I'd like that."

They ended the call, and Louise took the last bite of her bacon roll. She headed back to the bungalow.

A blast of cold air struck Louise in the face when she unlocked the front door. A brightness from the kitchen had invaded the inner hallway. Louise discarded her shopping and went to investigate. The back door of the bungalow was wide open and swinging in the coastal breeze. Louise froze. She was sure she had left the rear door closed. What to do? Should she walk through the bungalow and risk an encounter with the intruder? The front doorbell rang.

Louise crept out through the back door and tiptoed round to the front. Bob was pressing the bell.

"Bob?"

He turned and looked at her.

"Are you okay? You look like you've seen a ghost."

"Perhaps I have. I've been out and I think someone may have broken in while I was away."

"How do you know? Is anything missing?"

"I came home and found the back door wide open. I'm sure I left it locked."

Bob gave her a sceptical look.

"Have you checked if anything has been taken?"

"I was frightened. I didn't want to go back in."

"Come on. I'll look with you."

Bob limped to the back of the house and entered the kitchen.

"Hello? Burglar? Are you here?"

Louise began to feel foolish. She followed Bob, as he moved from room to room and checked the windows. There was no sign of damage. They ended their examination in the lounge. Louise noticed the front of the desk was open.

"I'm sure I left that closed."

Bob hobbled back into the kitchen and filled the kettle. Louise felt the return of old resentment at the way Bob made himself at home in her mother's house. He made two mugs of tea.

"Look, Lou, you've been under a lot of stress. You probably just left the back door open."

"But the desk was open."

"Has anything been taken from the desk?"

"No. I emptied it yesterday."

"That was quick work. What did you do with the papers?"

"In bags and boxes, ready to take back to the studio."

They sipped their tea.

"Lou, why don't you let me help you? This is a big task for one person alone."

Louise took back control.

"That's very kind of you, Bob, but I much prefer to work alone. Is that why you came… to offer help?"

"I was worried about you."

"I'm fine."

She picked up his empty mug, took it into the kitchen, then deliberately opened the front door and waited. He took the hint and walked slowly through the hallway. His legs didn't work as well as they used to, but he could still negotiate his way around reasonably flat areas. As he left the bungalow, he pecked her on the cheek.

"You take care," he said.

Louise shut the front door behind him, rubbed her cheek clean and watched Bob's car leave from the lounge window.

By lunchtime the following day, she had climbed into, and emptied, the loft and examined the contents of every drawer and cupboard. Precious items had been wrapped and boxed ready to load into her car. Two loads of the 'better' clothes and bric-a-brac had been taken to a local charity shop. She had even arranged to leave a spare key with a neighbour, turned the heating to low, and made a note of the energy meter readings. She went out to her car and pulled down the back seat. There would be plenty of room for the boxes and paintings.

"Just things," she said out loud to herself, as she turned her back on the bungalow. "Just a 'soon to be forgotten' shadow of a lifetime."

The bungalow doors and windows were double locked. Bins were emptied. Switches were turned off. Her car was loaded up, and she began the half-hour drive to her home in Robertsbridge.

193, Havelock Road,
Hastings,
East Sussex,
TN34 1BH
5th October 2016

Dear Mrs Watson,
Thank you for contacting us by telephone earlier this week. I can confirm that our valuer, Mr B Coggins, will be able to visit your late mother's bungalow on Thursday 6th October 2016. As agreed, he will collect the key from the neighbours, Mr and Mrs Brown, and return the key afterwards. I anticipate his visit will take a maximum of one hour. We will then write to you at your address in Robertsbridge with a written statement of the estimated value of goods to offset against our disposal costs. You may wish to leave a few items of furniture and curtains in situ while the bungalow is on the market.
We have already explained the evidence required as proof of probate.

Yours sincerely,
K Roberts and Son, House Clearance Specialists

TWO

Freshers' Week

Two months after her eleventh birthday Louise travelled three miles with Joan to Bishop's Stortford for her first day at Herts and Essex High School. The school was now a state-funded grammar school, but having previously been an all-girls, independent boarding school, it was still listed on the public school list. The all-female environment was steeped in tradition, and its nurturing environment was well suited to Louise's protected background. The beige and brown uniform had to be purchased from Daniel Neale's store in London. Girls wore gymslips for their first two years, after which their waists were considered suited to the dark brown block pleated skirts which were worn until the age of eighteen. Louise conformed without argument and was anxious to please her teachers.

Her first English lesson was timetabled for the second day.

"I want you to write about yourselves," explained the teacher, "At least three pages. Do your very best, so I know how good you are at writing. Tell me as much as you can about your home, your interests, and your background. Try to make your writing interesting by giving it a context. Describe your earliest memories, and how you feel about your family. Start now, and finish your essay for homework."

The teacher moved around the classroom and discussed the

writing with individual pupils. She noticed that Louise looked puzzled. "Do you have a problem, Louise?"

"Not really. It's just that I spent my first three years in Singapore, but I can't remember anything about it. Nothing at all. It's a shame, because I think it would be interesting to write about it."

"Perhaps your mother can jog your memory?" suggested the teacher, "Do you have any photographs?" Louise realised for the first time that Joan never spoke about Louise being in Singapore. She only ever talked about her own life there with Peter, Louise's father. She would ask her mother that evening.

After tea, Louise sat with her homework and asked her mother a question, "Have we got any photos of me in Singapore?"

Joan hesitated and then explained, "I'm sorry Louise, all our photos of you in Singapore were lost in the move back to England." Joan had used this excuse before with her own mother.

"Why are you asking?"

"We have to write an essay about ourselves for our English homework. I thought it would be interesting to say something about Singapore."

"I'm sorry, I can't help, Louise. You'll have to write about things you can remember." Louise accepted the explanation without question. She continued with her homework, while her mother went upstairs. Joan moved a chair in front of her large walnut wardrobe and climbed up to find a shoe box at the back of a top shelf. She steadied herself, as she lifted the box down and placed it on the bed. She retrieved a black and white photograph of a three-year old child with pigtails standing in front of a very large detached building with an ornate porch and sweeping drive. She kissed the photo and took it down to show Louise.

"This is the earliest photo I have of you. I can't remember where it was taken, but I think we had just returned to England from Singapore. That might be a hotel."

Louise laughed, "Look at my hair! And my old-fashioned clothes! Can I keep this photo, Mum?" Joan noticed that Louise no longer called her 'Mummy'.

"I think I'd better keep it for you. You can have it, when you are older." And Joan returned the photograph to its hiding place upstairs.

Louise was an excellent student. Having gained eight good 'O' levels, she moved into the Grammar School Sixth Form in Bishop's Stortford to study English, History and French. She had wanted to continue with her Art, but the school insisted that she was more suited to academic subjects. Her mother, Joan, had persuaded her that attending Art School would be a waste of her brain, and Louise reluctantly agreed. She secured a place to read English and Art History at Sussex University in Brighton, subject to reasonable 'A' level grades, which she easily achieved.

And so it was that at the end of September 1973, Joan and Peter loaded Louise's luggage into their car and transported her from the family home in Sawbridgeworth, Hertfordshire, to Brighton to install their daughter in one of the modern halls of residence at Sussex University. They helped Louise carry her suitcases up two flights of stairs to find her small single room with broken cupboard and undulating mattress. Louise took her parents for tea in the refectory. Joan reminded her daughter repeatedly about domestic necessities, and Louise listened to her mother with tolerance. Eventually Peter hinted to Joan that it was time to leave. Louise allowed her mother to hug her tearfully, before she watched in relief as both parents headed back to the car park.

A red-haired student with large brown eyes and wide shoulders moved over to sit next to Louise.

"It's hard for them to say goodbye, isn't it?"

"Just a bit," grinned Louise, "I'm Louise, by the way."

"Hi. My name's Gillian. I was here for part of last year, but I got glandular fever and missed two terms, so they're letting me repeat year one. What are you studying?"

"Art History and English."

"Great. I'm doing English and Sociology. We might share some lectures. It depends what tutor group they put you in. It's all up on the academic notice board in the central reception area. Would you like me to show you?"

"That would be brilliant."

The two young women stepped out of the refectory to take a tour of the spacious and thoughtfully landscaped campus. There were plenty of lawned areas, and the tree-lined internal roads were well signposted. Gillian took the lead, but even so, Louise felt a sudden sense of independence. Her future had begun.

They entered the main reception area and approached a large, well-organised, pinboard full of timetables. Louise made a note of her first week's lectures and tutorials and then allowed Gillian to show her the campus sights. There was a sports hall, a book shop and two large lecture theatres, as well as numerous smaller teaching spaces and social areas. Once the tour was over, a time was agreed to meet later in order to go to the student bar. Louise returned to her room and began to unpack. She put her clothes in the wardrobe and drawers and lined up her books on the window ledge. She used a large paper clip to support a temporary repair to the broken hinge on her wall cupboard. Her sketch pad and small palette with brushes were placed on the little desk. She searched the skirting board for a power point. Fortunately, there was one near the bed. Louise plugged in the little light which would comfort her night-times. She was relieved that electricity was included in the rent.

She pushed her suitcase under the bed and wandered into the corridor. The girl next door was sticking a massive brightly coloured poster from Athena on her bedroom wall. She stepped out into the corridor.

"Are we allowed to use sellotape on the walls?"

"Well it's a bit late to ask now," laughed Louise. The two girls introduced themselves, and Michelle was invited to join Louise and Gillian for their evening excursion to the bar.

After a swift supper in the refectory, Louise returned to her room. She changed into faded jeans and T-shirt and used her new heated tongs to style her hair into gentle blonde curls. She met up with Gillian and Michelle in the lobby. Michelle looked stunning in a tight-fitting low-cut T-shirt with satin trousers. Gillian, in contrast, had tied her beautiful red hair tightly back away from her face, which accentuated her wide cheeks and broad shoulders.

'Funny how we all like to look different,' thought Louise.

The student bar was packed out with freshers. Gillian led, as the girls fought their way to buy a drink. "You want a pint?" shouted Gillian.

Michelle and Louise nodded, assuming that pints were the accepted drink.

They grabbed their glasses from Gillian and moved to the side of the room. Clouds of cigarette smoke hung down from the ceiling, and the jukebox played 'Angie' by the Rolling Stones. Gillian offered Michelle and Louise a Rothman's. Michelle accepted, and Louise shook her head. She began to feel a little out of her depth. She gazed around the crowded room and imagined a watercolour painting full of smoky faces. "I must fit in," she told herself, but doubts began to invade her resolve.

Within ten minutes Gillian had passed to the other side of the room and was chatting to a group of young women. Michelle was being pursued by an attractive young man who smelled strongly of Brut aftershave. Louise was left alone watching the room. She felt uncomfortable, but was determined to stay.

She eventually decided to seek a few minutes' refuge in the ladies' toilet. Her mission to cross the room without spilling her half-full glass kept her focussed. She pushed open the outer toilet door and put her glass on the broken tiles of the window ledge.

'Half full or half empty?' Louise wondered, as she opened the inner door. Three girls were standing in front of the mirrors brushing their hair. Louise locked herself into a cubicle, then emerged and washed her hands in the sink. The green liquid soap had run out, and the blue roller towel was hanging loose from its housing. She shook her hands, then wiped them on her jeans to disperse the damp.

When she reached the outer area, her glass was still in place and waiting for her. Another girl came from the toilets, picked up a glass, and stood behind her.

"It's busy, isn't it?" said her companion, stating the obvious.

"Very," said Louise, "In fact I feel a bit overwhelmed."

"I'm so glad you said that. I thought it was just me."

The two young women stepped out of the entrance to the

toilet and took refuge under the porch overhang, just outside the student bar.

"What are you studying?"

"History and French."

"We probably won't meet up at lectures then," said Louise, but she felt strengthened by their one moment of shared understanding.

"I guess we had better go back in," they both agreed.

And each girl returned to their respective and separate places, glasses in hand.

THREE

Meeting Charlie

Despite a nervous start, Louise thrived at university. She had always been considered level-headed and capable of making mature decisions. Her inner calm and self-belief compensated for her sheltered upbringing. Although one of the younger students in her year, she quickly embraced both her new academic routine and her social life. She coped well with her studies and joined the university Art Society. She soon became familiar with the well-resourced art department, which was available for unlimited use by all student members of the society. She spent much of her free time exploring the variety of media, and took an optional extra class in watercolour painting. The flirtatious older male tutor would regularly tell the class that Louise's paintings floated off the paper just like Louise. Although somewhat more eloquent, he reminded her of her childhood companion, Bob, and Louise kept him at a distance.

Louise and Gillian became firm friends. They would travel by bus into Brighton together and rummage through the sales to make their grants stretch further. Gillian had passed her driving test, and, with the help of wages from a part-time job in a sports shop, managed to run a small car for more distant journeys. Louise and her 'arty' friends, as Gillian called them, would persuade Gillian to run them to Ditchling Beacon where they would sit on the hillside and sketch the views. Gillian secretly told Louise that she preferred girls to boys. There being little sensible publicity about gender preferences in the 1970s, Louise believed that Gillian was just going through a phase.

Her other friend, Michelle, was, by contrast, a man hunter. She dressed in tight-fitting clothes to show off her sexuality and was often absent from her room in the morning after an evening's dancing. Louise's strict upbringing prevented her from entirely approving of Michelle's lifestyle, but she envied the freedom which allowed Michelle to launch herself into a succession of unconstrained physical relationships. Louise was hugely admired by the male students at the university. Her tall willowy figure and long blonde curls suited the mid-seventies fashions, and heads turned whenever she passed through the campus. However, her good looks did not immediately translate into boyfriends. She had a slightly aloof air which kept all but the most adventurous suitors at a distance. As a result, Louise found herself being pursued only by the more courageous, but often insensitive and immature, young men who she frequently rejected. "Are you sure you don't prefer girls?" Gillian asked more than once.

"I do like men," Louise would always reply. "I just haven't found the right one yet."

During her first year Louise dutifully returned home for each vacation. Joan and Peter would come and collect her in their car, and, at the end of each holiday, drive her back to university with boxes full of cake and bags full of clean washing. Much to Joan's dismay, Louise moved out of hall for her second year and shared a rundown flat with Gillian and Michelle.

"You're not allowed to stay in hall in year two, Mum. That's reserved for first years."

Joan worried how Louise would cope, but Peter reminded his wife that Louise would soon be twenty.

"I hate to tell you this Joan, but Louise is a grown up, and very capable. Despite your best efforts to stop her, she has turned into a mature young woman."

Joan sighed, "I do know really."

Just before the first half term of year two, Louise plucked up the courage to tell her mother she would not be coming home. Instead she would be visiting friends for the holiday. She had been invited to stay with Michelle, who promised her dances and outings in the company of her older brother and his friends. They caught the train to Polegate, where Michelle's brother, Charlie, picked them up from the station. He was about five years older than Michelle, medium height and full of charm.

"Well, what have we here, Michelle? You didn't tell me you were bringing such a beauty to stay. I'm going to have problems leaving the house to go to work."

"Stop talking such flannel, Charlie. Louise is my friend, and very refined. She doesn't need to be flattered by you."

Michelle was secretly pleased that Charlie liked her friend. She looked up to her older brother and wanted his approval. Charlie lifted Louise's case into the boot, and let Michelle put her own case on top. "Thanks for your help, brother dear."

"Gotta get my priorities right," Charlie lifted one eyebrow and winked at Michelle. Louise climbed into the back of the car before Charlie could stop her. Michelle laughed and sat in the front next to her brother. He accelerated as fast as he could and drove at speed to the family home in Willingdon just outside of Eastbourne. It was a large detached house with a circular drive and was decorated in, what Joan would call, slightly ostentatious style. Michelle's mother came out to meet them. She hugged Michelle, and then Louise, and led the girls into the house leaving Charlie to deal with the cases. The house was immaculately clean and filled with display cases of porcelain dolls and collectable figures. Louise winced slightly at the décor. "What a beautiful house, Mrs Windsor."

"Please call me Mandy."

Mandy led the girls to a first-floor bedroom. There were two single beds with matching floral duvets, ornate built-in wardrobes and a large extravagant kidney-shaped dressing table with gilt mirror.

"I thought you would both prefer to share the same room."

Mandy was pleased she had decided to put Michelle and

Louise in together. Louise was a very attractive young woman, and she wouldn't entirely have trusted her son if Louise had been left to sleep on her own.

Louise looked round the bedroom and smiled. Everything in the house was matching and modern, but chosen in what her mother would call rather pretentious fashion. Joan's childhood on the family-farm estate followed by eight years as an expat wife had indoctrinated her into a strictly class-led, understated system of taste. Louise suspected that both Joan and Peter would regard the Windsors as 'new rich'.

'Ironic,' thought Louise, 'With a surname like Windsor.'

The week passed quickly. Michelle had obviously been given a lot more freedom than Louise, encouraged by her parents. Despite being slightly overweight, Mandy dressed in tight-fitting polyester knitwear, which revealed her cleavage, and her father ('you must call me Stewart') poured excessively strong gin and tonics for the two girls at every opportunity.

"You'll get Louise drunk, Stewart," laughed Mandy, "I don't think she's used to our extravagant ways."

"It's fine, Mandy. I'm having a good time. I admit my mum is pretty strict, but I'm a grown up now and I am allowed to enjoy myself."

"I would be happy to show you how to be even more grown up," interrupted Charlie.

"You keep your hands off her," instructed Stewart jovially. Louise had entered a world which was so different to her own, and she found the contrast very alluring. Louise also began to understand why Michelle behaved with so much less inhibition than she did.

Charlie flirted with Louise and showed her considerable attention and charm. He was enormously attracted to her, but realised that he would need to plan his conquest with care. Louise was also Michelle's friend, and he didn't want to upset his younger sister. He took the girls to a disco in Eastbourne, where they met up with some of Charlie's friends. He drove them to the seafront. They paddled in the sea beside the pier and ate extravagant sundaes in an Italian ice cream parlour. On the final evening Charlie took Louise and Michelle for a meal at a local pub. "Several of my mates will be there, and I want to impress them. Come on Louise, take my arm."

Louise happily agreed, and Charlie showed her off to his friends, pretending she was his girlfriend. At dinner, he more than once put his hand on her knee, and each time she removed it, but not with any great rush, Charlie noted.

When Louise and Michelle left for Brighton, Mandy threw her arms around Louise. "You are such a lovely girl, Louise. You are welcome any time."

Stewart ran them to the station. Charlie and his mother watched them leave. "You could do a lot worse, Charlie," said Mandy. "She's a nice girl, got class. She would be a great asset with your bosses, and I suspect she would keep you in order."

Charlie grinned at his mother, "I might pop down to Brighton in a couple of weeks' time." Charlie had scraped through university, leaving with a third-class degree in Business Studies. However, he interviewed well and had nevertheless easily secured a place on a graduate training programme with a popular car manufacturer. Always destined for a career in sales, he was quickly promoted. By the time he met Louise, he had already been promoted to a junior executive post with a company car. Louise was fascinated by Charlie. She instinctively knew that he liked her, but was unsure how much. She was attracted to his slightly dangerous personality. She wanted to tame him. She suspected he might be a philanderer, the sort of man her mother would call 'a collector of women'.

Although the 1960s had a reputation for sexual liberation, this alleged freedom had not translated into reality for the majority of people. It was not until the early 1970s when sexual behaviour really began to change. Once the contraceptive pill finally became available to unmarried women, fear of pregnancy outside of marriage began to diminish. Many quite conventional couples then chose to live together before marriage. Louise was a part of this new generation, and she did not feel the need to save her virginity for marriage. However, she had no intention of being too free with her sexual favours. Until she encountered Charlie, she had not met a man with whom she wished to be very intimate. Charlie's hand on her knee had finally aroused undiscovered feelings deep within her. When two weeks later, Michelle told Louise that Charlie intended to stay with them for the weekend, Louise experienced a somersault within.

"I'll shove a sleeping bag on the sofa," said Michelle, "We'll make him slum it."

Charlie arrived after work at 7 pm on the Friday. He sat with the three flatmates and ate their home-made spaghetti bolognaise. He praised their cooking and waited patiently to accompany them to the student bar. On arrival at the bar, Gillian headed towards her group of female friends, leaving Michelle and Louise to entertain Charlie. Charlie put some money in the jukebox and waited for his choice of record to be played. Eventually the familiar voices of 'The Carpenters' filled the room and slowed down the pace of dancing. Charlie invited Louise to dance. He pulled her close, gripped her hips, and made good use of the slow rhythm to feel the length of her body pressed against his own. Louise noticed that Michelle was dancing with another male student and no longer felt guilty about deserting her friend. At the end of the dance, Charlie suggested that he and Louise should take a walk outside. He lit up a cigarette and put his other arm around her.

"Are you cold?"

"No, I'm fine."

He finished his cigarette, and led her into a study room doorway. He blocked her exit with his body and held the back of her head. His other hand pushed gently into her spine and moved slowly down her back. His kiss was long and penetrating. Louise disliked the taste of cigarette, but was soon overtaken by inward passion. Her previous experiences were few enough for her to be taken completely by surprise at the strength of her desire.

"You are so beautiful." He kissed her again.

She began to shiver, and they returned to the bar. Back at the flat Louise's head began to swim. "I'm sorry, the drink has gone to my head. I need to lie down."

Charlie had never intended to sleep with Louise on the first night, so was able to play the perfect gentleman and tuck her up in bed with a bucket.

The following day, after a late start, Charlie drove the three students into Brighton. They wandered along the seafront and took a stroll up West Pier. Gillian and Michelle walked on ahead, while Charlie sauntered at a slower pace with Louise. "Are you feeling better now?"

"Yes, I'm perfectly okay now. It was self-inflicted anyway. I don't deserve any sympathy."

Charlie laughed. "We've all done it, Louise. It's part of growing up."

She felt slightly patronised. He took her hand as they walked. "What do you think you'll do when you've finished at Uni?"

"I'd like to paint full time, but there's very little money in it. I'll probably end up teaching."

"There's not a lot of money in teaching either, but it's a good job for a woman." Charlie turned the conversation round to his own career, giving a long description of his promotion, prospects and salary. Louise couldn't help but be impressed.

"I was thinking that I might whisk you away from the others tonight. We could go out for a meal, just you and me."

"That sounds great."

"I'll go and book a table now."

Charlie disappeared and joined the group half an hour later. "All sorted."

At 8 pm that night Charlie and Louise found themselves sitting at a table for two in a seafront hotel in Brighton sharing dinner and drinking wine. Charlie confessed to Louise that he would have to return to Eastbourne the following day. "I'm based in Tunbridge Wells, but I have a training course in The Midlands next week. I'm going to miss you."

"Work has to come first."

"I should be able to visit again in about three weeks. Would you like that?"

"Yes, I would."

Charlie sighed. "I'm hanging on to every last moment with you, Louise. Once we get back to the flat we'll be overtaken by Michelle… and the sexy Gillian!" Louise felt unkind, but she laughed.

He pretended to be deep in thought, "We could stay here, you know. I'm sure they would have space. We could drink champagne and be Mr and Mrs Smith." Charlie failed to add that he had already booked a double room that morning.

Louise thought quickly. Would she ever get another such luxurious offer for the loss of her virginity? She looked Charlie straight in the eye. "I'm a virgin."

"I guessed. You wait here, Mrs Smith, I'll be back in a minute."

Charlie returned very rapidly with a room key and a cheap bottle of sparkling wine. He led Louise by the hand to the lift. They quickly found the fourth-floor bedroom, where, filled with desire, she allowed him to unpeel the clothes from her body. Charlie was an experienced lover, and he ensured that Louise's initiation into fully-developed sexual activity was both exciting and free from anxiety. He wanted to leave her wanting more, to keep her for himself, and intended, over time, to educate her slowly into his more self-centred desires.

Neither Gillian or Michelle said a word when Charlie and Louise returned to the flat the following morning. Louise walked straight past them and into her room. Charlie sat in the living room on the sofa and lit up a cigarette. "Any chance of a coffee?"

"I'll get it," said Michelle.

Gillian knocked on Louise's door. "Can I come in?"

"Yes." Louise had changed back into her jeans.

"Are you okay?"

"I'm fine."

"How was it?"

"None of your business," Louise grinned.

Charlie drank his coffee and joined Gillian in Louise's bedroom.

"Shall I go?" asked Gillian.

"No, you stay."

Charlie kissed Louise. "I have to leave. Ring me on Friday evening. I'll see you in three weeks' time."

The relationship between Charlie and Louise developed slowly. Charlie would visit every three weeks, stay overnight and take Louise out for meals and treats. For the rest of the time she remained faithful to him, and concentrated on her painting and her studies. She spent a lot of time with Gillian and her friends. Charlie rarely witnessed Louise's occasional nightmares, and he accepted her need for a nightlight. He was naturally self-centred, but, in his own unimaginative way, he cared for Louise. In early summer Charlie took Louise on holiday to Cornwall. She took an extra case full of paints and sketch pads, but was allowed little time by Charlie to pursue her hobby. Although disappointed that he did not understand or respect her love of painting, Louise considered herself lucky to have Charlie's affection. She had spent several weekends at his parents' house in Willingdon, and found the contrast with her own family refreshing. She arranged to take Charlie to meet Joan and Peter after their trip to Cornwall. She took the time to brief Charlie on the family 'standards', before he was introduced. Louise was worried that they might think Charlie a bit beneath her, but Charlie was a born performer and he charmed her parents. When he drove her back to Brighton afterwards he set aside his charm and spent the entire journey criticising Joan and Peter. "How can they live in that dingy house with all those old things?"

"They're called antiques."

"Well I hope you won't want all that old stuff in our house." It was a passing comment, but Louise noticed its meaning.

"You don't look a bit like them. Are you sure they are related to you?"

"'Fraid so, Charlie, I'm stuck with them."

"Their house must be worth a packet."

"I believe it is, and my mother inherited a share of the farming estate, which was sold after grandpa died."

"So you'll be worth loads when they've gone."

"You're wicked, Charlie. I never think about it. I love my parents very much."

"And I will learn to love them as well."

Shortly before Louise graduated, Charlie secretly drove to Hertfordshire and asked Peter's permission to marry Louise. "Have you actually asked her?" inquired Peter.

"No, I'm asking you first."

"I only want my daughter to be happy. If Louise agrees, then you have my blessing."

Charlie presented Louise with an overly large engagement ring on her twenty-first birthday. He never doubted that she would accept, and was taken by surprise when Louise asked for some time to think about it. Her hesitation startled him, and his face fell.

"I can't live without you, Louise. You are the most beautiful woman in the world, and I want everyone to see that you belong to me."

"I'm not a possession, Charlie."

"It's just my way of talking. I will give you everything you need. Please say 'yes'," he begged.

"We can't get married until I've qualified as a teacher." Charlie approved of Louise's plan to teach. It was a career which would fit in well with raising a family.

"Is that a yes then? A wedding in the Summer of 1977, the largest, most fancy wedding in the South of England."

"It will be understated and classy, Charlie. My parents will want to organise the wedding," Louise smiled, "Our wedding."

"Say it then, tell me."

"I will marry you, Charlie Windsor."

They began to make plans.

Charlie wanted an extravagant engagement party in Eastbourne, but Louise refused. She would need to spend time revising for her education exams, and wanted the space to concentrate.

"You're good at exams, Louise, you don't need to revise."

"I'm good at exams, because I do revise."

Charlie gave in. It was important for his future wife to have academic success. He agreed to Joan's proposal of a family afternoon tea at The Royal Victoria Hotel in Brighton. This would be an opportunity for both sets of parents to meet. Charlie stressed to his mother the importance of dressing conservatively, and she purchased a pink cashmere twinset especially for the occasion. She accessorised the outfit with a large pair of hanging ruby earrings, and the unconventional contrast was, by sheer chance, remarkably compelling. Joan's dress sense appeared, in contrast, old fashioned and dowdy. Her pear-shaped body had sagged with middle age. She couldn't help but be impressed by Mandy's appearance. Nevertheless, the conversation between the two mothers was polite rather than flowing. The two fathers were simply anxious to survive the afternoon. They instinctively knew that there was potential for conflict between their respective wives, and they were determined to protect themselves and, more especially, the newly-engaged couple.

"What did you think?" Joan asked Peter on the journey home.

"Not really my types," he admitted, "New rich, but the world is changing. Class doesn't carry much weight these days. Money speaks. I guess they'll do."

Peter decided not to add that he had found Mandy enormously attractive.

FOUR

Marriage, Divorce and Relocation

Michelle, Gillian and Louise had always assumed that they would vacate the student flat after graduation. Michelle had met a recently-divorced, Italian business man who owned a chain of prestigious restaurants in London. He offered Michelle a job in his personnel department, and invited her to live with him in his penthouse in Richmond. Luigi was in his forties. Mandy and Stewart were concerned at the age gap, but, as always, they allowed their daughter to learn from her mistakes without comment. Luigi and one of his staff arrived at the flat at the end of June and helped Michelle empty her university life into a white catering van. The three girls hugged, before Michelle disappeared towards the road to London and her new existence. Gillian, however, had decided to stay in Brighton and secured a placement as a trainee social worker based in one of the East Sussex Social Services Departments. Louise also had chosen to remain at Sussex University to take the one year postgraduate qualification as a teacher. So Gillian and Louise renewed the lease on the flat for one more year. With exams to pass in educational studies and two long teaching practices at local comprehensive schools, Louise was grateful for the continuity in her domestic arrangements. She coped easily with the academic side of her studies, but found the practical aspects of teaching more demanding. Her young students challenged her authority, and Louise began to doubt whether she had the ability to grasp the essentials of classroom discipline. She started to wonder if she would ever properly control a class of teenagers. Early in her final teaching practice, her mentor, who was also the Deputy Head, called her to a meeting.

"Louise, I've been watching you. You have an amazing presence around the school, and your colleagues respect you. When you enter the staffroom, heads turn, and people listen to you. You have a natural charisma and slightly elusive manner which is perfect for teaching. But when you enter a classroom, you doubt your ability. You lose confidence and your charisma disappears. I think you have one very small problem, which is causing you major difficulties." He paused before speaking, "You must believe in yourself, and be yourself. Parade your inner confidence in front of the kids. They won't undermine you unless they see you are afraid. You have the potential to be a great teacher... one of the very best."

Louise reflected on her mentor's advice. His words floated around in her mind. "You have the potential to be a great teacher... one of the best." She rang Charlie and told him about her conversation with the Deputy Head.

"He probably fancies you," Charlie responded. Louise was disappointed by his flippancy, but it strengthened her resolve to be a good teacher.

Later that evening she told Gillian about her mentor and about Charlie's response.

"Don't let Charlie belittle you, Louise. You are far cleverer than he is. He has personality, but very little brain. Remember that. You must prove to him that you are more than just blonde hair and long legs."

The following morning, Louise took a deep breath and walked in to a classroom to teach her most challenging set of pupils. She was determined to prove to Charlie that she could be a good teacher. The students immediately recognised her renewed confidence and responded with respect. Louise built on that one successful moment to further increase her confidence. She had turned a corner in her professional development. The Deputy Head walked past her classroom, glanced in, and smiled. He had been right about Louise.

Charlie married Louise in the Summer of 1977, after she qualified with distinction as a teacher. Louise had predicted that her parents would insist on organising and paying for the wedding, and so it was. The Church of England ceremony was followed by a reception in an expensive, but traditional, hotel in Hatfield. As part of their preparation, Charlie and Louise had been required to meet with the local vicar and discuss their future.

They gathered together the necessary paperwork and handed it to the clergyman.

"Oh, a shortened birth certificate… no mention of parents or place of birth," commented the vicar to Louise. "I don't often see one of these."

"I was born in Singapore," explained Louise.

"That probably accounts for it," replied the vicar.

The wedding passed without incident. Gillian and Michelle were both bridesmaids dressed in deep blue satin gowns with leg of mutton sleeves. Michelle had wanted to wear crimson, but Louise chose a colour which would not clash with Gillian's vivid red hair. Despite Charlie's objections, Louise stayed with her parents for a whole month before the wedding. She delighted her mother by modelling the simple oyster-white wedding dress which she had chosen for her special day. The classical design, accessorised with a deep blue bouquet of trailing blooms, though not especially fashionable for the late seventies, suited Louise's willowy figure and lightly curled long hair. The contrast between Louise and the rest of Joan's family was yet again very apparent, and Louise's entrance in the Church silenced the congregation into admiration. Despite his mother's opinion that Louise had chosen far too simple a design for her dress, Charlie looked at his bride to be with pride. He had indeed been clever to capture such an attractive prize.

The reception ran perfectly to plan. Peter made a heartfelt speech in which he extolled the virtues of his daughter. Charlie made a humorous speech with occasional innuendo about his sex-life with Louise. Mandy flirted with Luigi and hinted that the role of bridesmaid was traditionally a precursor to another wedding.

Charlie and Louise purchased a brand-new, semi-detached house near Tunbridge Wells, close to where Charlie worked. Louise secured a teaching post at a secondary school nearby and embarked on a successful career teaching English, History and Art. She had a lively personality and, with her renewed confidence, related well to her students. She was rapidly promoted to Head of Department. The additional salary soon enabled the young married couple to mortgage themselves into a large detached house ten miles north of Robertsbridge in East Sussex. Michelle visited regularly and, a few years later, stayed with the married couple for several weeks, after she parted company with Luigi.

Gillian found Charlie irritating, but kept up her friendship with Louise. Louise and Gillian would ring each other every few weeks. Several years later, Louise had an unexpected extra phone call from Gillian.

"Hi Gillian, how's the job?" Gillian was now a senior social worker in Brighton.

"The job's fine, but that's not why I'm phoning. I've got to tell someone. I have fallen in love."

"At last! I'll ring you back in an hour. Charlie will be watching football, and we can have a good gossip."

Louise phoned back as promised.

"Tell me all about her then."

"Her name is Catherine. She's two years older than me, and she's a nursing sister at the Royal Sussex Hospital in Brighton. She likes me to look feminine. She has long dark hair, she is kind and funny, and she looks stunning in her nurse's uniform."

"Too much information, Gillian."

"Sorry. We met at a social services training course on child protection. We are buying a flat together in Brighton."

"I am so pleased for you, Gillian. You've taken your time,

but it sounds like you've found your ideal partner. I wish I'd taken a bit more time to find mine."

"Things not going well?"

"Oh, you know, it's okay. I don't ask what he does when he goes away on his so-called business trips. I said that to Mandy once, and she implied that a man only strays, if his wife can't satisfy him. She never criticises Michelle, but she is a cow to me sometimes. So when am I going to meet Catherine?"

"As soon as we've moved, I'll invite you over to see our new flat."

"That sounds lovely. I will look forward to it."

Much to Mandy's disappointment, the longed for grandchildren had never appeared, so Louise consoled herself by concentrating on her career. The early novelty of the difference between her parents and her in-laws soon wore off, not helped by Mandy's occasional hints that Louise was somehow deficient by not producing an heir. Charlie began to spend more frequent nights away on business, and Louise converted the childless fourth bedroom into a temporary art studio. She compensated for her growing loneliness by spending her evenings painting large swirling watercolours. Charlie disliked the mess, but was impressed with the extra income generated by the sales of her pictures. Over the years his earnings and prospects had fluctuated with the fortunes of the UK car industry, and they were both grateful for the constancy of Louise's more secure income as a teacher.

When Louise was in her late thirties, the local comprehensive school in Robertsbridge set up a locally-based behaviour unit with additional outreach to nearby primary schools. The curriculum would still cover the basics, but there would be more emphasis on vocational studies and practical work. Louise was now recognised for her ability to deal with more challenging students, and had long been a source of pastoral support for less-experienced colleagues. With her love of English, and her creative abilities, she was the ideal candidate to head up the new unit. She was interviewed and appointed as Head of Centre and received a salary commensurate with her new responsibilities. Charlie wanted them to move again to a larger, more prestigious property, but, by this time, Louise was beginning to doubt whether their marriage would survive. She refused to move again, began to set aside a proportion of her salary into a personal savings account, and to work towards greater financial independence. Charlie seemed neither to notice or care.

A few years after the millennium, the behaviour unit's host school converted to an Academy. The political climate had changed, and the centre was instructed to concentrate more fully on a traditional, less creative, curriculum. Louise struggled to make the more rigorous system work for her, often damaged, students, and she disliked the increasing pressure of her new target-driven role. Eventually the centre fell victim to severe education cuts, and was closed. Louise was offered voluntary redundancy with an enhanced pension in her late fifties, which she gratefully accepted. She taught watercolours part-time at local evening classes for a couple more years and then retired fully to concentrate on her own painting.

Peter had retired from the Civil Service three years after Louise got married. He and Joan spent ten happy retirement years together with frequent holidays abroad, including one return visit to Singapore. Sadly, just after his seventieth birthday Peter began to develop a persistent cough. After two severe throat infections and a bout of bronchitis he noticed his breathing was becoming laboured. Despite his diplomatic training, which discouraged the discussion of personal ailments, Peter paid a long overdue visit to his GP. An immediate referral to the hospital was followed by a chest x-ray. The consultant showed Peter the large patch on his lung, which was diagnosed as malignant. The blame was placed on years of diplomatic cigars and London pollution. After one series of radiotherapy, the malignancy slowed down, but so did Peter, not helped by a succession of chest infections which eventually turned into pneumonia. He died in 1994.

The following year, Joan, whose own parents had passed away some years previously, decided to break her ties with Hertfordshire and move to the coast. She bought a bungalow in the East Sussex village of Fairlight. It was a picturesque rural community which nestled on the cliff top between Hastings and Rye. The location was close enough to Tunbridge Wells for Joan to visit Louise and Charlie, and she hoped to tempt Louise to stay with the prospect of sea views which demanded to be painted. Much to Louise's surprise, Joan sold most of the antique furniture and replaced it with Parker Knoll, Ercol, and floral carpets and curtains. 'My dad would be horrified,' thought Louise, though not unkindly. Peter had always been the master of the house, and that had included the family taste in décor.

Despite the frequent mists which would suddenly descend over the cliff, Louise visited her mother with her artist's kit often in the first years after Joan relocated. The internal walls of Joan's bungalow in Fairlight, and those of her neighbours, were soon covered in framed original watercolours of local scenery signed by Louise Windsor.

Louise finally divorced Charlie two years after her father died. No longer constrained by the strict shadow of Peter's diplomatic service morals, Louise felt free to make all her own choices. She knew that Charlie had been unfaithful to her more than once. She wanted to paint, to visit her mother more frequently, and to hold a conversation which did not centre around sales targets and impressing colleagues. There were no children in the marriage to hold it together, and she had sufficient income and potential pension to ensure her independence. Charlie made no objections, when Louise finally told him she wanted a divorce. He simply shrugged his shoulders and said, "If that's what you want."

They eventually came to a financial agreement. Louise reverted to the surname 'Watson', but kept the title 'Mrs', which she preferred to 'Ms'. Within three months of the divorce Charlie had traded Louise in for a younger, more fashionable model. "Good thing we have no children," Louise confessed to Gillian. "I fear that Charlie's new wife is about to eat into his assets."

Michelle had proved a useful go-between during the pre-divorce negotiations, but once they were no longer married,

Louise's friendship with Michelle faded away, until it consisted only of an annual Christmas card.

Bob had lived in Sawbridgeworth most of his life. As a child he had resided a few doors away from Joan, Peter and Louise. After he left home, he purchased a small flat of his own in Sawbridgeworth town centre and stayed in contact with Joan and Peter. When Peter became ill, Joan would invite Bob for a weekly Sunday lunch, and Peter was grateful that his wife had some company. Two years after Joan moved to Fairlight, Bob retired and purchased a semi-detached house in Hastings. Property in Hastings was far less expensive than in the Hertfordshire commuter belt, so Bob was able to afford the larger property. He never invited Joan or Louise to visit his new home, but his weekly Sunday lunches with Joan were soon reinstated.

Catherine and Gillian legalised their relationship with a partnership ceremony some years after Louise split up with Charlie. Louise was asked to be a witness, and Louise and Joan travelled together to the registry office in Brighton. Although Joan was known for her traditional views, unlike many women of her age, she was perfectly at ease with the idea of Gillian having a female partner. "It's the diplomatic service that does it," she explained to Louise, "It gives you a very broad view of the world. Very little surprises me these days."

Louise was grateful for her mother's company, and relieved not to have Charlie sneering at Gillian behind her back.

FIVE

After Joan

Louise's studio was located on the top two floors of a wooden-clad, listed building in the village of Robertsbridge. The property had been an indulgent post-divorce purchase, of which her mother disapproved. Although Joan was enormously proud of her daughter's artistic talent, she had never come to terms with Louise's slightly bohemian tastes.

"What's wrong with a nice modern flat with sea views? You could do lovely paintings from there, and you don't have a man any more to help you with maintenance. They have some really spacious, new apartments on the outskirts of Hastings. You'll soon be fed up with those stairs. You're not getting any younger."

Louise smiled indulgently at Joan and ignored her. Her mother was right about the stairs, but Louise was buying a lifestyle and a view. As well as containing an en suite double bedroom, the top floor of her new home housed a large, open-plan, studio area with full-length windows on two sides. The room made full use of available light, and was a perfect retreat for a painter. Buying the studio was a final rejection of her time with Charlie, and it was good value. Mortgages on listed buildings were difficult to obtain, but, with a small subsidy from her late-father's estate, Louise was a cash buyer.

After years of hard work, Louise had converted the two-storey apartment into a beautifully refurbished home with lounge, kitchen, two bedrooms and bathroom on the lower floor and a very spacious open-plan art studio/living area and en suite double bedroom on the upper floor. The changing views across the Sussex countryside from the large top-floor windows were breathtaking.

Louise arrived home after her weekend clearing Joan's bungalow and parked her car behind the flat. She unlocked the front door and sighed at the number of boxes which would need to be carried up three flights of stairs to her home. She wondered whether she would dare to try and persuade her downstairs neighbours, Frank and Doreen, to sell the rest of the house to her. Joan's bungalow would surely fetch enough money for her to make the purchase.

Louise climbed the stairs holding a small box in her arms. "One box every trip," she mumbled. She left the box in her hallway and ascended to the studio. The afternoon autumn sunshine flooded into the room. It was good to be home. Although the kitchen and the living room were on the lower floor, Louise spent most of her time in the studio. She had created a small sitting area in addition to the central wooden farmhouse-style table and chairs. There was a kitchenette with a kettle and coffee maker on the worktop and a fridge beside the butler sink. The draining board had designated spaces for paintbrushes, pots and coffee mugs. With the kettle filled and boiling, Louise dropped into a chair and observed her surroundings. She wanted to plan the rest of her life, but could not envisage a sufficiently large block of time.

'Small steps, Louise,' she told herself, 'One week at a time.'

She walked into her bedroom and looked at her reflection in the full-length mirror. Louise was tall and slim, and the stairs at the flat had kept her fit. She had always been proud of her appearance. With the help of highlights, her hair still gave the impression of being effortlessly blonde. She looked young for her sixty-one years. That day, however, she noticed the tiredness on her face. Every line and shadow seemed to be exaggerated. The strain of the past weeks was showing. She needed to take some time for herself. Tea consumed, she grabbed several sturdy shopping bags and headed back downstairs. The small supermarket nearby was open, and she purchased some provisions. Leaving the remaining empty bags in her car, she re-entered the flat with a bag of shopping and a bag of paperwork. As darkness began to fall, she illuminated every room in the flat.

Most people who knew Louise regarded her as capable and independent. They envied her apparent self-contained nature and her ability to live alone. Louise did not perceive herself in this way. She emitted a calm and confident façade which disguised her loneliness. She was only content with her own company when immersed in her watercolour painting. She spent the rest of her time on planned busyness to compensate for being alone. It was fear of loneliness which had helped to keep her with Charlie for so many years.

She disliked the dark and always turned lights on in every part of her home. "Don't you worry about your electricity bill?" Joan would frequently ask.

"It used to be a problem, Mum, but not any more. These energy saving bulbs are very cheap to run."

Once her evening meal was eaten, Louise sat in the brightly-lit studio with a glass of wine. She telephoned her friend, Gillian.

"Are you busy? I felt like a chat."

"No, not busy at all. Catherine is away for two weeks. I'm on my own. How's it going?"

"It's a bit odd, not having Mum to chat to on the phone... and to worry about, but the bungalow is more or less sorted."

"You are so efficient, Louise. It took me months to sort out Dad's house, when he died."

"You wouldn't say I was efficient, if you saw my car. It's still loaded with boxes."

"Well don't try carrying too much at once. The stairs at your flat are treacherous, and you need to look after your back."

"I know, I know. Gillian, can I come and stay for a few days?"

"Of course, lovely, you are welcome any time, especially while Catherine is away."

SIX

Visiting Gillian

Gillian now lived with her partner, Catherine, in a converted flat close to 'The Lanes' in Brighton. When Louise had finally split up with Charlie after many years of marriage, distant acquaintances wondered if Louise was also gay, about to evict Catherine and to move in with Gillian. Those who knew Louise well did not, for a moment, believe this. Louise projected a form of femininity, which was unconsciously, but entirely, heterosexual.

Three days after Louise's return from sorting out her mother's bungalow, she had finally emptied her car. She filled it once more with two small suitcases, a watercolour painting, and a large bunch of flowers to make the promised visit to Gillian. It was about an hour's drive to Brighton. Catherine was away on a training course, and Louise was able to use her allocated parking space. She arrived mid-afternoon, and was tempted to wander round 'The Lanes' before entering Gillian's flat. However, she knew Gillian was anxious to see her and could feel Joan's etiquette lecture in her head, 'Visitors should always arrive punctually.'

Louise resisted the temptation of 'The Lanes' and knocked at the door. Gillian looked relaxed and unkempt without Catherine to impress.

"It's so good to see you. Let me take your case."

Gillian lifted the heaviest of the luggage up the short, second, flight of stairs, while Louise placed the flowers in the kitchen sink and took her painting into the living area.

"I've got to show you something, Lou, can you come up?"

Louise rolled her eyes and climbed the stairs to the spare bedroom. Gillian was pointing to a power point next to the bed.

"Look, it's a movement activated night light, or you can leave it on all night. I bought it especially for you."

"Aw… that is so thoughtful, Gillian. I might be able to turn my torch off!" Louise paused momentarily, "Which reminds me, I had a very odd experience at Mum's house. I must tell you about it."

Time may have aged their faces and their energy levels, but it had not diminished their friendship. Within an hour, the two ex-students were sitting together in a bistro, drinking wine and waiting for food.

"Are you absolutely sure you left the back door locked? You might simply have forgotten. You had just buried your mum."

"I'm positive. And I'm also certain I left the desk closed. You know me, I'm paranoid about that sort of stuff. I'm telling you, if Bob hadn't turned up, I might still be there. I was petrified."

"Bob does have his uses then?"

"He's a creep, but, yes, I was relieved to see him."

"And you're sure nothing was missing?"

"Nothing at all."

"Perhaps it was kids? The postman? A fox?"

"A fox who can open the front of a desk… that's a bit Disney!" And both girls giggled.

The mystery had not been solved, but the wine had lessened its importance.

After a shared starter of ribs and chicken strips followed by two pasta dishes washed down with house red, they walked the short distance back to Gillian's flat.

Gillian produced her laptop and, fired by alcohol, began to assert herself.

"How long is it now, since you and Charlie parted company?"

Louise did a sum in her head.

"Nineteen years."

"And since then, apart from a couple of disastrous one-night stands, you've turned into a Victorian maiden aunt. It's gone on long enough, Louise. You have no ties any more. It's time to try online dating."

Louise felt an unexpected flutter of excitement. "For God's sake, Gillian, do I have to?"

"Yes, you do, and I am entirely impartial about men, so I can advise you. But first, I need to find my specs, so top up our wine, and I will be back."

Louise refilled their glasses from a second bottle and grabbed the laptop. She did a search for online dating. 'Senior's Dating' was thrown up as the first option.

"You have got to be joking," said Gillian, as she sat down beside Louise and looked at the screen.

"It might be a good place to start."

"Dirty old men, more like," Gillian sighed. "Okay, call this a trial run."

Senior's Dating is a service exclusively for professionals aged fifty and over. We recognise that the most successful relationships tend to be formed between people of similar ages and backgrounds. SPECIAL OFFER… Ladies up to the age of sixty-five can have free full membership for twelve months.

Click here to find your ideal partner…

"Told you, it's full of dirty old men. They have to bribe the women with free membership."

Louise ignored her best friend and began to fill in the form.
Name… Louise

"You can't call yourself by your real name!" exclaimed Gillian.

"Okay, I'll be… Elouise. Is that okay?" The phone rang. It was Catherine, and Gillian disappeared into the kitchen. Louise finished the form somewhat flippantly and clicked the 'send' button before Gillian returned.

"Right, let's fill in your profile."

"Too late, I've already done it."

"Can I see?"

"No."

"Spoilsport, what about a photo?"

"I found one on the cloud and used that."

"I hope you made yourself look sexy. Men expect it, you know."

"Gillian, I'm sixty-one years old. They will have to like me, as I am, or not at all."

SEVEN

Senior's Dating

Simon was spending yet another Saturday evening alone. He divided his attention between *Strictly Come Dancing* and Facebook. When the *Strictly* theme tune became too persistent, he rose from his chair to boil the kettle. He lifted the almost empty bottle of wine into a cupboard to prevent himself from finishing it. 'So little self-control,' he mused, 'That I have to hide things from myself.'

In many ways, Simon was used to being self-reliant. His mother had died when he was in his early teens, and he had been left in the care of his well-meaning, but disorganised father. Simon had rapidly learned to take on many of the domestic tasks, previously assigned to his mother. He had a strong bond with his father, but was often, by necessity, left alone to look after himself. He had compensated for his solitary existence by spending a disproportionate amount of time with his technical drawing board, learning about the early developments in computer technology and design, which had predated the first wave of home computers. His father had been relieved, when university threw Simon back into a wider social environment, and his son fell in love with a succession of girlfriends. His father was therefore surprised that Simon didn't find a wife while at university. He worried that Simon had developed a rather idealised and outdated view of women, brought about by the untimely death of his mother. Simon's final choice of Julie to be his wife some years later tended to confirm this. His pretty young wife was an accomplished homemaker, but not a great thinker. Simon instinctively knew his father had been concerned. However, the arrival of two grandsons had drawn the whole family together. Simon was pleased his divorce with Julie had happened after his father died. He would not have enjoyed explaining a situation, which Simon perceived as partly his own fault. He refused to forgive Julie, and had insisted on the divorce, but he hated living alone. It brought back all the unwelcome memories of his solitary teenage years. He was well able to look after himself, but he needed to feel loved.

With mug of tea in hand, he grabbed his reading glasses and returned to his laptop. A new advert had appeared at the top of his Facebook page.

Meet Senior Singles in Your Area

'I suppose it makes a change from funeral plan adverts,' thought Simon, and he clicked on the link.

"Come on then, find me an old lady to date!" he spoke out loud to his computer.

Senior's Dating is a service exclusively for professionals aged fifty and over. We recognise that the most successful relationships tend to be formed between people of similar ages and backgrounds.

Click here to find your ideal partner…

Simon clicked.

He filled in the boxes.

Age range fifty to seventy, male, heterosexual, retired website designer, self-employed. Area, Sussex, Surrey, Kent.

He pressed enter.

Several female faces appeared on his screen. Simon scrolled through the photos.

"Too old, too plastic, too ugly… God, Simon, you are so shallow. Keep looking."

He finally selected two appealing faces for further consideration.

Name Clarissa. Widow, retired civil servant. Interests dog walking, religion….

"Religion, no thank you."

He made one last try.

Name Elouise. Non-smoker, Divorced, Retired teacher. Interests, painting, theatre.

He lifted his hands from the keyboard and looked at her photo again.

"Maybe."

He clicked for more details.

In order to see this member's full profile and access the exciting world of Senior's Dating, you need to pay the introductory fee and register as a full member.

He pressed the back key to return to her picture. A different set of faces had appeared.

"Dammit. They've got me."

He registered and paid the £25 fee.

We recommend that you take time to fill in your profile details and include a recent photo. This is how our thousands of members will find you. In the meantime, feel free to browse and search our member gallery.

He clicked 'search by name'.

Search for Elouise… twenty-six profiles with name Elouise.

Narrow search by area…

Sussex, Surrey, Kent… three profiles.

"Found her!"

Hi. My name is Elouise, well it isn't really, but you're not supposed to give your real name, and you have to write something. I used to be a teacher of English and Art, but now I am retired. I have purchased a small studio and I spend a lot of time painting watercolours. I live in East Sussex, about ten miles from the coast.

Simon clicked '*save to favourites*' on her name.

He googled a map of the Sussex coast. Lewes, Hailsham, Battle even? He wondered where she lived.

He returned to her profile. She looked vaguely familiar.

He searched for a relevant FAQ.

Q. *What happens if I find someone I know?*

A. *We have thousands of members, so this is very unlikely. If you think you know someone we suggest you move on to a different profile.*

Simon decided to ignore this advice.

Q. *How many profiles should I contact?*

A. *We would recommend at least five. Our members, especially the women, are often in demand, so you probably won't get to meet the first profile that appeals to you.*

Q. *How do I make contact with a member?*

A. *Once you have filled in your own profile, you can choose to send it to up to ten members at a time. If they agree to make contact, the site will open up a chat box between you.*

EIGHT

Contact

Despite pressure from Gillian, Louise chose not to initiate contact with anyone on the Senior's Dating site, while she was staying in Brighton. The women spent two very enjoyable evenings perusing male profiles and giggling, but Louise would not agree to take the matter further. She felt a bit guilty about the way she and Gillian were poking fun at the profiles. Their favourite phrase became "Own teeth or falsies?" and then they would erupt into fits of laughter. Louise was adamant that she would only chat to someone, if he made the first contact. However, she did secretly feel disappointed when she heard nothing for the following two days. Then, unexpectedly, she noticed an email from Senior's Dating on the Saturday morning, just as she was loading her car to leave Brighton.

Congratulations. Your profile is now live on the Senior's Dating Site. Within the next forty-eight hours you will receive details of any members who have asked to make contact with you.

Good luck, and Happy Dating!

Gillian noticed that Louise was stood by her car reading the screen of her phone.

"Is everything okay?"

"Yes fine. It's just an update from the house-clearance people. I'll deal with it when I get home."

Within five minutes, Louise was on her way. She left the main A27 at Lewes and chose to take a more rural route via Ringmer and Hailsham. She drove along country roads as far as Battle, then headed north to Robertsbridge. The trees were just beginning to show the first signs of their October colours, and Louise became engrossed in an imagined watercolour palette of autumn shades. She was home by mid-morning.

Once more she climbed the staircase to her studio with a suitcase in each hand. 'I'd better find a man with a strong back,' she joked with herself.

She delayed turning on her computer for as long as she could by unpacking her case, sorting the washing, loading the washing machine and opening her mail. There was indeed a letter from the House Clearance Company. They offered a small payment as balance after clearance. Louise knew she should really get a second quote, but she didn't want the trouble. She would deal with it later.

With coffee and a sandwich on the table in front of her, she finally switched on her laptop and reread in detail the email from Senior's Dating. There was a list of recommendations for personal safety when making contact, and a warning not to be disappointed if only a few names requested contact. She began to regret allowing Gillian and two bottles of wine to tempt her into completing the profile form. When no email arrived the following day, she felt even more despondent. She occupied herself for the rest of her Sunday by mixing palettes of red and gold colours inspired by her drive back from Brighton. When there was still no message in her inbox at the end of the weekend, she assumed that no one was interested in her. Her night time was filled with dreams of rejection and hands pulling her away from loved ones. She was relieved to wake up. Her buzzing phone told her that it was Monday morning, and an email was waiting. It was from Senior's Dating.

Since your profile went live forty-eight hours ago, the following members have requested to make contact with you. You can click on their profiles below.

There was a list of twenty-three men.

"Cripes!"

The twenty-three names were each listed with a very short summary.

John, sixty-five, separated, retired teacher, location Lewes

Stephen, sixty-seven, divorced, builder, location Hastings

Malcolm, sixty-two, widower, accountant, location Tunbridge Wells

Chris, sixty-nine, divorced, retired engineer, location Bexhill

And that was just the first four! Louise decided it would take her ages to work through the entire list of twenty-three names. She clicked on John's name. A photo of an overweight man smiling with crooked teeth popped up on her screen. She cringed, and then felt guilty for giving so much importance to a photograph. She needed a way to help her to decide how to order the profiles. She grabbed a piece of paper and wrote notes.

'Age… must be sixty-five or under. Worried that someone older might need a carer before too long.

Location… preferably within ten miles. Don't want to travel too far.

Marital status… disregard separated, too much possible baggage. Divorced okay. Widower, too much to live up to.

Photograph… try not to take into account, but no tattoos.'

It was a start.

None of the first four names fitted her criteria, but out of twenty-three names she found three possibles.

Graham, sixty-three, non-smoker, divorced, retired Maths teacher, Hastings

Philip, sixty, non-smoker, divorced, estate agent, Bexhill

Simon, sixty-two, non-smoker, divorced, retired website designer, Battle

Louise clicked on each profile in order.

Graham ('nice photo', she thought, ignoring her own guidelines.) He was wearing a pale blue, short-sleeved shirt and had a gentle smile. She read his 'About Me' paragraph.

Hi, I'm Graham. I took early retirement from teaching for mental health reasons two years ago. Actually, I think they were desperate to get rid of me anyway. My divorce came through six months ago, so

I'm trying to get my life back together. I'm hoping someone on this site can help me. I like pubs, takeaways, and sixties music.

Louise didn't read any more. "Sorry Graham, I appreciate your honesty, but I want to be a date, not a therapist."

Philip (very smart photo of a neat man in a well-tailored suit and tie)

My name is Philip, and I own a chain of estate agents along the South Coast. I am hoping to hand the business over to my son in the next few years. I own a large bungalow in Bexhill, and a villa in Southern Spain. I was divorced several years ago and am looking for someone to share my retirement with.

'Different,' thought Louise. 'It would be fun to paint watercolours in Spain. I wonder if I am well enough appointed or considered in need of refurbishment?' She kept Philip on the list.

Simon (good looking in photo, interesting face, but photo could be deceptive)

I'm Simon, a retired website designer, though I still do a bit of part-time work for ex-clients. I like exploring new places, walking and eating out. I am pretty easy-going really. I enjoy seeing my sons and grandchild, and I keep busy, but I miss female company. It's lonely living on your own. I own a house in Battle.

'Difficult to say about this one,' Louise said to herself. 'What does easy-going mean, I wonder?'

She left Simon on the list.

Without looking any more, she closed her computer, and went for a walk through the village. She stopped for a baguette at 'The Ostrich'. Sam, the barman, greeted her. "Hi Louise, you been away? I haven't seen you for ages."

I stayed at Mum's after the funeral, and then went to Brighton to stay with Gillian for a couple of days."

"Oh, of course, sorry, I forgot about your mum. How did it go?"

"It was okay, you know how it is." And Sam turned to serve another customer, while Louise sat on her own and ate her lunch. She suddenly felt very isolated and longed to be able to telephone her mother. Fearful that a tear might appear on her cheek, she soon left the pub and returned to her studio. She switched on her computer and returned to the email from Senior's Dating. She clicked the link **ALLOW CONTACT** for Philip and Simon.

Feeling a mixture of emotions, Louise decided to calm her nerves by starting a new painting. She imagined a Spanish village of whitewashed houses and orange groves and used a soft pencil to outline the scene onto a large sheet of cartridge paper attached to an easel. She added two chickens and a stray donkey meandering down the cobbled street.

"If only…"

NINE

The Estate Agent

Philip had sent a contact request to five women in Senior's Dating. Louise was the oldest. He had promised himself the company of a younger woman, but had been attracted by Louise's photograph.

'Always good to diversify,' he told himself. He had complete confidence in his ability to attract a new woman. Almost by instinct, he tried a slightly different approach with each of his targets. He decided to be very direct with the 'older woman', Elouise.

Hi. It's Philip here. You clicked the 'enable contact' button on my profile on the Dating Website. There is a smart new restaurant which has recently opened on Bexhill seafront, and I would like to take you there for lunch. When would be a good time to ring you?

'Well he doesn't waste time,' thought Louise. 'Obviously used to closing a sale without argument.'

It was a long time, since a man had bought her lunch. 'Bexhill-on-Sea, hardly a den of wickedness,' she smiled to herself, and she was flattered by the quick response. She sent Philip her phone number and said she would be in from 7 pm.

Simon's first message arrived early on the same afternoon.

Dear Elouise,

Thank you for allowing me to make contact with you. I feel I should tell you a bit more about myself, but I'm not sure what to say. I see you paint watercolours. I am terribly ignorant about painting, but willing to learn. I did my degree in graphic design, which was pretty progressive for the 70s, but not at all artistic. We created images by using straight lines, geometric shapes and mathematical angles. I do hope you reply. Would there be a good time to catch you on 'chat'?

With kind regards,
Simon

Louise read Simon's message several times. She revisited his profile picture and tried to imagine him sitting at his computer. She began to think about composing a reply. The phone rang.

"Elouise? It's Philip. I know I'm early, but I couldn't wait to talk to you."

"Oh, hi. It's Louise by the way."

"Are you busy this Sunday? I've got a viewing with a client at 11.30, and we could meet for lunch after."

'So he can have another viewing,' Louise laughed to herself.

"Just a minute, Philip, I need to check." She glanced at the blank calendar on the studio wall.

"Sunday is fine. Where do you want to meet?"

"Do you know Bexhill?"

"Yes, my mum used to live in Fairlight, and I often took her to the De La Warr Pavilion for tea."

"Let's meet in the Pavilion foyer then, just outside where they have all those odd art exhibitions. Say 12.15? I'll book a table at Merton's for 12.30."

"That sounds nice. How will I recognise you?"

"I'll be the guy in a suit. See you then." And he put the phone down. Louise dialled 1471 and wrote down the number. She texted Gillian.

I'VE GOT A DATE

GO LOUISE! Came the almost instant reply.

The phone rang again. Louise was worried it might be Philip. 'I hope he doesn't hassle me,' she thought.

It was Gillian. "Come on then, tell me all about him."

"There's not a lot to tell really. He's an estate agent. He seems to know nothing about art. I think he wants to check if I am in need of refurbishment."

Both girls giggled. Louise explained about his profile, the short phone call, and Philip's direct approach.

"He's probably used to dealing like that in his business. You will invite me over to Spain won't you, when you move in together?"

"Ha, ha, very funny. Seriously, Gillian, do you think I'll be safe?"

"You're meeting in a public place. He's hardly likely to try and assault you in the De La Warr Pavilion foyer. Give me the phone number, I'll check it out for you. Might be worth looking up the restaurant on Trip Advisor, as well. Look I've got to go. Catherine will be home in a minute, and I promised her a special tea. I'll email you."

Louise went straight to Trip Advisor.

Merton's Restaurant on Bexhill Seafront: Modern cuisine with a twist 4.5 stars

'*Amazing food, but rather expensive for lunch,*' said the first reviewer.

'I suppose he will offer to pay, but I'd better take some cash just in case. I hope he doesn't expect anything back from his investment'. She spent the next half hour wondering what to wear.

Gillian's short email reassured her.

The phone number is for Sussex Estates in Bexhill. It's an independent chain of Estate Agents with five branches. The owner is a Mr Philip Travers. All looks legit. Gx

Louise looked up Sussex Estates on her computer. There was a staged photograph of Philip Travers and three female negotiators outside a branch in Seaford. He was smart, but not tall. The suited saleswomen in their high heels rather overshadowed him. Suddenly, Louise realised that she had completely forgotten about Simon.

Sunday soon arrived. Louise dressed carefully trying to look effortlessly smart. She wore a plain, dark green, long-sleeved dress which showed off her hair, and a smart winter coat. She chose flat shoes, not being sure of his height. Philip was ten minutes late. Louise watched him climb the short staircase at the entrance to the De La Warr Pavilion and step into the foyer. He was shorter than average, almost petite and immaculately dressed in a tailored grey suit with a deep blue tie. He spotted her immediately and approached her with confidence. He took her hand and kissed it with a flamboyant air.

"You are even more beautiful than your photograph. Sorry I'm late. The buyer wouldn't stop talking. I hope you are hungry. The food in Merton's is very good."

They crossed the road and walked towards the restaurant. An over-attentive waiter took Louise's coat. He showed them to a window table, which overlooked the sea. Drinks were quickly ordered, and menus placed on the table. Louise noticed that the waiter kept withdrawing into the back of the restaurant to cough discreetly into a tissue. She hoped he wasn't infectious.

"Choose whatever you want," instructed Philip. "I have an account. It's all tax deductible."

'Nice to know,' thought Louise. Somehow eating a tax-deductible meal felt a little too businesslike. Philip told her about his clients, how he had grown his chain of offices, and his plans for the future. He described his house in Spain, recommended different dishes on the menu, and made a point of addressing the waiter by his first name. His phone rang twice during the meal, and he made no attempt to mute his voice, so as not to disturb the other diners. Louise enjoyed the food, and was genuinely interested in everything he told her. She wondered when Philip would ask her about herself. By the time they reached the dessert, she realised that he was a far more accomplished talker than listener. Louise could concentrate on eating, as she would not be required to talk, apart from the occasional nod of agreement. She tried to imagine how Philip coped when asking clients to describe their accommodation preferences, and eventually came to the conclusion that he probably told his clients what they needed, and they were persuaded by his self-confidence. He was articulate, intelligent, and very self-centred. She tried not to compare him with Charlie, but the similarities kept confronting her. After the meal, he invited her to take a walk along the promenade.

"I am expecting a couple more calls, but I could fit in a walk," he offered.

Louise refused on the grounds that she had arranged to meet a friend later that afternoon. "You really need to concentrate on your business, Philip. I wouldn't want to distract you." Her sarcasm went unnoticed.

TEN

Talking to Simon

Simon's mail from Senior's Dating had arrived on the previous Monday afternoon. He had been at a client's house in Sedlescombe updating an agricultural-foodstuffs website. The client noticed Simon repeatedly checking his phone.

"Is everything alright, Simon?"

"Yes, of course, sorry. I'm just expecting to hear from a friend after a hospital appointment."

Simon put his phone in his pocket, gave his full attention back to the client's computer screen and priced up the last of the sacks of grain.

He packed up slowly so as not to appear hurried.

"I hope that's you sorted. Any problems let me know, will you? I'll send you my invoice."

And Simon was soon in his car driving back to his house in Battle.

He drove slowly up Battle High Street past the Abbey towards the main roundabout. A left turn and sharp right led him to the entrance to his drive. He parked his car at a careless angle outside his house and unlocked the front door. He warmed up his computer while the kettle was filled and beginning to boil.

He read the email from Senior's Dating.

Senior's Dating Update

Congratulations. Our client, 'Elouise', has enabled contact with you after reading your profile.

You now have two options.

1. You can send our client an introductory message with more details about yourself.

2. If you see a blue dot by our client's name on your account page, you can chat directly.

Simon clicked on his account page. He looked at the page layout and was impressed with the website design. Sadly, there was no blue dot. He opened 'word' and began to draft a message.

Dear Elouise,

Thank you for allowing me to make contact with you. I feel I should tell you a bit more about myself, but I'm not sure what to say.

A sudden thought overwhelmed him... talk about her... not yourself.

I see you paint watercolours. I am terribly ignorant about painting, but very willing to learn. I did my degree in graphic design, which was pretty progressive for the 70s, but we dealt in straight lines and mathematical angles. You have beautiful eyes... he deleted the last four words... I do hope you reply. Would there be a good time to catch you on 'chat'?

Simon felt sick. He edited his post one last time and pressed 'send'.

Louise finally made contact with Simon on the day before she had lunch with Philip. She felt very disloyal to both of them, though Gillian had reassured her that making multiple contacts on an internet dating site was not considered to be two-timing. She had been flustered by Philip's direct approach on the Friday and felt unprepared for a date. When she finally replied to Simon on the Saturday morning, she said she would be unavailable to 'chat' until the following Tuesday. She couldn't cope with the idea of building a relationship with more than one man at a time.

Louise had woken early on the Monday morning after her lunch with Philip. She felt disappointed and needed to rationalise her thoughts. She made herself a coffee, turned on her computer and signed in to Senior's Dating. Simon's name popped up in a chat box.

"I know you said Tuesday, but I noticed you were online. Is now a good time to chat?"

Louise felt herself blush. *"Yes, now is a very good time to chat. I'm just drinking a coffee."*

"Filter or instant?" The ordinariness of his question amused Louise.

"Instant. I'll make a proper pot of filter later, before I start painting."

"What are you painting? Is that a correct question to ask when someone is painting?"

"I had started a rural street scene in Spain, but I've given up now. I think I'll do something autumnal."

Simon tried to imagine Elouise in her studio surrounded by canvases and paint brushes. He wanted to ask what she wore when she painted, but thought that might sound a bit of an intrusive question.

"Will you paint all day?"

"Probably not. I'll stop mid-morning, and then go out for a sandwich. It will break up the day." Louise worried that she had made herself appear lonely. Simon felt more hopeful.

"Have you been on this site long?"

"No, just a few days, it's all a bit odd somehow."

"The words 'Senior's Dating' put me off a bit." Simon risked a joke, *"You haven't got a zimmer frame, have you?"* He suddenly felt anxious. What if she really did have a zimmer frame?

Louise laughed, *"No zimmer frame, just aching legs when I climb the three flights of stairs to my studio."*

A second chat box opened. It was Philip.

"Hello Louise, I just wanted to say how much I enjoyed yesterday. I do hope we can do it again."

"Simon, I'm sorry, the phone's ringing I have to go. My name is Louise by the way. I would like to chat again."

"Philip, yes lunch was delicious. Look sorry the phone is ringing, I can't chat now. I'll get back to you."

Louise came out of chat. She needed to learn how to cut off a conversation. You can only invent a certain number of phone calls.

She got dressed, made a pot of coffee and began to paint... and think.

Louise's style of painting changed with her mood. This morning's effort was a quickly executed flurry of autumn colours with a faint trace of distant blue hope. She stepped back and regarded the painting. She couldn't decide if it was a complete mess or an example of spontaneous genius. She would revisit it later.

After a swift sandwich in 'The Ostrich', she hurried back and wrote several drafts of a message to Philip, before clicking 'send'.

> *Dear Philip,*
>
> *It was lovely to meet you yesterday, and to hear all about your business and your plans for the future. The food in the restaurant was excellent, and it was very kind of you to insist on paying.*
>
> *As you know, I have only recently joined Senior's Dating and I am still finding my feet. I don't think I am ready yet to start a serious relationship, so it would be fairer to you, if we didn't meet up again.*
>
> *I do hope you find a suitable match.*
>
> *With best wishes,*
>
> *Louise*

The reply came back quickly.

> *Dear Louise,*
>
> *Thank you for your message. I am very disappointed, as I have always wanted to be seen with a slim blonde on my arm. However, I do understand.*
>
> *If ever you need the services of an estate agent, I would be more than happy to quote you beneficial terms.*
>
> *Kind regards,*
>
> *Philip*

Louise smiled. 'I just might take you up on that offer, Philip Travers!'

Louise clicked '*disable* contact' by Philp's name. She felt a bit mean, but was not prepared to take the chance of him popping up unexpectedly in the chat area. She noticed that Simon was online, and decided to risk further contact.

"*Sorry I cut you off suddenly this morning. The phone was only from a call centre, but, by the time I realised, it was too late… you had disappeared.*"

"*I thought I might have upset you with my zimmer frame comment.*"
"*Oh no, you made me laugh!*"
"*Did you finish your painting?… How long does a painting take?*"
"*Anything from five minutes to several years. Yes, I finished it.*"
"*Are you pleased with it?*"

"*I'm not sure. I can't decide if it's a masterpiece or a complete mess.*"

"*You could send me a photo. I can't paint at all, so I would think it was wonderful.*"

Louise began to like Simon's online personality. He had a gentle humour which charmed her.

"*Louise, I realise this question is something of a cliché, but is it possible we've met before? Your photo looked familiar.*"

"*I'm afraid I didn't recognise your photo, and my visual memory is pretty good. Perhaps you've seen me somewhere locally? You live in Battle, don't you?*"

"*Yes, do you go to Battle a lot?*"

"*Hardly ever, I'm afraid to say, but I do like Battle. It's a beautiful town.*" Louise tried to think where Simon might have seen her.

"*I live in Robertsbridge. I have a friend in Brighton who I often visit. My mum used to live in Fairlight.*"

Simon paused, "*I'm thinking. No, I can't think where I have seen you.*" He struggled to continue the conversation. He didn't want her to go, but neither did he want to appear too pushy.

"*What have you got planned for the rest of your day?*"

"*Not much. I might ring my friend Gillian in Brighton… I've known Gillian since university. She's gay, but I'm not, in case you were wondering.*"

Simon smiled. She was losing coherence, so there was just a chance she wanted to please him. He hoped she would be like this, if he got the chance to meet her.

"*So is there a queue?*"
"*A queue for what?*"

"A queue for people who are allowed to phone you?"

Louise was aware that he was starting to flirt with her. She felt a lift to her spirits.

"I am an ex-teacher. You have to form an orderly line."

"Can I have your phone number, please, Miss?"

"I'll think about it," and Louise playfully closed the conversation.

Within a few minutes she had messaged Simon her home number. She expected the phone to ring straight away, but it didn't. Instead another chat box opened.

"Louise, I've just remembered where I saw you. You were walking away from a funeral in Fairlight. A man from your group came and spoke to me while he smoked a cigarette."

"Yes, that was me. And the man would be Karen's husband, Michael. Karen is my cousin, though I used to call her Auntie Karen."

"Was it the funeral of someone close?"

"My mother. She died four weeks ago."

"I'm sorry."

"So am I. I miss her terribly. I am still sorting her bungalow."

"Can I ring you tonight?"

"Yes, of course."

The talk of a death had banished any further flirting. Simon tried to remember the willowy female shape which he had spotted in the distance close to Fairlight Church. He wondered if a mother's passing felt different, if you were adopted.

Simon was nervous about the phone call. He wanted to ask to meet Louise, but was worried she might say 'no'. It had been three years since he split up with Julie, and he felt out of practice at talking to women. He decided to eat some dinner and then make the call. The packet lasagne took ten minutes in the microwave and emerged congealed.

'Oh to have a meal cooked for me… but I mustn't say that. It's sexist,' he told himself. Simon was a good cook, but rarely prepared proper food for himself, now he lived alone. He poured himself a glass of wine and gulped down the processed pasta. The phone was on the table beside him. He picked up his handwritten note with Louise's number on it.

"For god's sake, man, just ring her!"

He keyed in Louise's number.

"Hello?"

"It's Simon."

"Oh hi. Thank you for ringing. Did you have a good supper?" Simon liked her voice, and Louise instantly realised she had just asked a really mundane question.

"Packet lasagne. I'm afraid I don't look after myself so well now I'm on my own. I bet you cooked yourself something fresh." Simon instantly realised he had just replied with a really mundane answer.

"I forced myself to make a stir fry," said Louise, "I will eat the rest tomorrow." She wanted to say how much she hated eating alone, but it smacked of self-pity, so she changed the subject.

"What were you doing in Fairlight on the day of my mum's funeral?"

"I'd been to Rye market, for a wander, as you do, and I stopped for a cuppa on the way back. I had intended to walk in the Firehills on the clifftop, but it started to rain. You and few others were wandering away from the Church."

"Did you have a long chat with Michael?"

"Just a few words. He was obviously desperate for a cigarette."

"That sounds like Michael. It was a very long service. The vicar went on and on… you know how they do, all about Mum's history and salvation etc. It was good to catch up with family though. We went on to 'The Lodge' for refreshments, tea and sandwiches."

"Have you always lived in Sussex?"

"No, I spent my childhood in Hertfordshire, but I was born in Singapore. My dad was in the diplomatic service. We returned to England when I was three."

Simon began to wonder if Louise's birth parents were natives of Singapore. That didn't make sense though. Louise was blonde… at least he thought she was.

"I went to Sussex University in Brighton, and stayed down here for my PGCE. After that I lived near Tunbridge Wells until my divorce. Mum moved to Fairlight after my dad died. What about you?"

"I come from a Sussex family. My parents owned a house in Westfield until they died. I moved to Ninfield with my ex-wife, when we married. One of my sons still lives with her in Ninfield. Do you have children?"

"Sadly no. It just never happened. At least it made my marriage break up a bit easier."

"How long have you been on your own?"

"Nineteen years. Dad died shortly before I split up with Charlie, so I've spent most of my time looking out for my mum."

The conversation began to slow. Simon found it hard to imagine how anyone could survive so long on their own. She might be very set in her ways, then again she was an artist. Weren't artists meant to be a bit chaotic? His thoughts were rambling. It was difficult to turn the conversation around to a lighter subject. Eventually, Simon took the lead.

"I was wondering, would you like to meet up? I mean you don't have to, if you don't want to… or you think it's too soon."

"I would love to meet up," replied Louise

"When shall we meet then? Where would you like to go?"

Louise thought. There were plenty of lovely rural pubs between Robertsbridge and Battle, but she knew that, for her safety, a first meeting ought to be somewhere reasonably busy and not too remote. "I realise this is an odd suggestion, Simon, but what about the Garden Centre in Sedlescombe? There's a coffee shop there."

"Do you have a garden?"

Louise laughed, "No, but I can dream."

"Garden Centre it is then."

A meeting was agreed for 11 am in two days' time.

Louise fell into a deep dreamless sleep. But just after midnight she woke in a sweat. Her arms felt heavy, and there was a dull throb inside her head. She took a gulp of water and realised that her throat felt gritty and swollen. She carefully moved her feet onto the floor of the bedroom. As she began to stand, the room seemed to float around her. She sat down on the edge of the bed. Her throbbing head was sending painful waves above her eyes. She stood up carefully and took the few unsteady steps to the bathroom. She returned with a jug of water, a thermometer and two paracetamol. Her temperature was 38.5. She slid under the bedclothes and fell back into an intermittent sleep. By the time the morning sunshine invaded the room, she could feel a stabbing sharpness in her throat, and an irritating and persistent cough. She felt miserably ill and depressed with a growing awareness that she would have to cancel, no postpone, her meeting with Simon. She was fearful that he might think she was somehow messing him around. She managed to make herself a hot, drink, grabbed her laptop, and crawled back to bed.

Simon woke with a feeling optimism. He rose early and walked into Battle for a coffee and breakfast. A familiar car passed him, and a child waved through the window. He recognised his granddaughter and daughter-in-law on the daily school run and waved back. By the time he arrived back home, it was 10 am. The phone rang. It was his older son, Joe, ringing from work.

"I hear you were looking very perky this morning. Caroline said you almost danced into town."

"Sometimes I think you are monitoring me by CCTV."

"Well if you insist on bouncing into town at school-run time… So come on Dad, tell me what's made you so happy?"

"Actually, Joe, you are not entitled to know all my secrets. I'll tell you in a few days."

Simon finished the call.

Joe phoned his wife back. "You're right. He's in a very good mood, but he wouldn't say why. Maybe he's booked a holiday."

"Maybe he's got a girlfriend," Caroline challenged her husband.

"I very much doubt it. He's still nursing his hurt about Mum. At least I think he is."

"Would you mind, if he found someone else?"

Joe thought for a moment. "No, I don't think I'd mind. It would be a good thing. As long as the lady wasn't after his money, or tried to interfere in our lives. I still think it's unlikely though. Must go now, Caroline, I have an appointment."

"And I need to go to work."

Caroline had recently increased her hours as a part-time accounts assistant and was still adjusting to her new routine.

Simon turned on his computer. There was a message from Louise.

Dear Simon,

I am so so sorry…

Simon hesitated, fearful to read on.

I have woken up this morning with a temperature and a wicked sore throat. Would you mind if we postponed our meeting for a few days? I don't want to pass my germs on to you. I am really sorry.

Best wishes Louise.

Simon felt despondent. He didn't want to doubt her, but he wondered if Louise had changed her mind.

Dear Louise,

I'm sorry that you are unwell. There are a lot of nasty bugs around at the moment. Let me know when you feel better and we can reschedule.

Kind regards,

Simon

He reread the sent message and thought it sounded unsympathetic, so added in a second message.

PS Do you need anything?

Louise would have loved a visit from someone who would bring her endless hot drinks and sympathy, but she certainly didn't want to be seen. Her hair was already suffering from her high temperature, and she couldn't stop coughing. She felt exhausted and depressed. Tears began to slide down her cheeks. She barely had the energy to wipe them away. She acknowledged that her body was paying her back for the anguish of the past few weeks. She buried herself under the bedclothes and cried herself to sleep. Her inflated temperature induced an endless stream of dreams.

She would find herself alone in the dark with paintings of farm animals circling around her throbbing head. Gillian appeared and separated her fingers from grasping an easel full of wet-painted paper. Philip took her by the hand and dragged her towards a large group of waiters who were coughing into the seafront waves. The heat of her body burned away at the virus, as she lay in bed unable to sit up. Eventually, after two days, of restless dreaming, the searing temperature began to subside. Louise woke, relieved that her nightmares were over. The headache had gone, but the remnants of a cough were clearing her chest from the last of any infection. She knew from experience that it would take several more days for a full recovery. She dragged her failing limbs into the studio and boiled the kettle. It took two journeys for her to carry her hot drink and her laptop back into the bedroom. There were two unanswered messages from Simon asking how she was. She began to type.

Dear Simon,

I'm really sorry that I didn't reply earlier to your messages. I have been asleep, on and off, for almost two days, but I am beginning to feel better. Please believe me, I don't get ill often, but I think Mum's death and everything just caught up with me, and the bug or virus or whatever it was took possession of me. Perhaps we could agree a date to meet in a week's time, when I am sure I will be fully recovered? I want to enjoy our first meeting, not be coughing all the time. I didn't have a flu jab this year, and I am now regretting it.

With very best wishes,

Louise

Simon had convinced himself that Louise was not interested. When the message arrived, he expected it to tell him that she didn't want to meet him after all. He finally persuaded himself to click on her name in his inbox. He read the message several times. These were not the words of someone who didn't want to meet him. These were the words of someone who had been genuinely ill. However hard he tried to doubt her, he was convinced that she had been really unwell. He began to feel guilty.

"Can I ring you?" He saw she was online.

"Yes, as long as you don't mind me coughing down the phone."

"Can I catch your germs over the phone?"

"I'm sure you can. I expect I am horribly contagious."

"I'll risk it."

Louise's phone rang. She picked up the handset and coughed. "Sorry about the cough. Is that you Simon?"

"No, it's the doctor, I'm officially prescribing a flu jab for you next year."

"You don't have to tell me. I have suffered enough. Simon, I'm so pleased to hear from you. I am so so sorry I had to postpone our meeting. I was worried that you might think I had changed my mind."

"It never occurred to me," Simon lied. "Have you got everything you need? Can I do some shopping for you?"

Louise was very tempted to say 'yes'. However, she knew she shouldn't give him her address, and, in any case, she looked awful. Her vanity was enough to overcome her need for a visit.

"I'm fine. The infection is beginning to subside, so I can get as far as the fridge." She was beginning to lose her voice.

"Louise, you are getting hoarse. I'm going to hang up now. Before I go, can I have your mobile number? Then I can text you." Louise croaked her mobile number down the phone.

Simon had a brainwave and found the book of Christmas cracker jokes, which he used to amuse his granddaughter, Sophie. If he couldn't make Louise better, he would try and make her laugh.

What do you get if you eat Christmas decorations? He texted.

I don't know, came the reply.

Tinselitis.

Louise laughed out loud and then coughed. She was enjoying Simon's distant company. Each day he would text a joke and make a short phone call.

What is Rudolph's favourite time of the year?

Tell me.

Red Nose Day.

Groan.

When Simon phoned the following day, Louise sounded much better. "Are you enjoying my jokes?" he asked.

"No, they are terrible, but well actually yes, they have kept me sane."

"You know how to stop the jokes, don't you?"

"How?"

"Agree to meet me at the Garden Centre on Wednesday."

"What time?"

"11 am."

"I'll be there."

Louise looked in the mirror and rang the hairdressers. She managed to make an appointment.

ELEVEN

The Garden Centre

It was only a short drive from Robertsbridge to Sedlescombe. The garden centre was located off the main A21, a short distance from the village. Louise arrived early and parked her car in a remote space hoping to spot Simon arrive. She was not disappointed. He had given her his car registration, and the black Mercedes drove into the car park a few minutes later. She watched him climb out of his car and look around. He was tall with broad shoulders and a thinning hairline.

She watched him walk to the entrance and then back to his car.

'Time to go.' She got out of her Astra and walked towards him. Simon soon spotted Louise as she strode towards him. He remembered the lines of her body, as he watched her approach. "Louise?"

"Hi," she felt herself blush. "We made it then."

He smiled broadly. She liked his face.

He wanted to hug her, but lost confidence. "At least the sun is shining. Are you feeling completely better now?"

"Almost completely."

"Well you must say, if you need to rest."

"I will, Simon." Louise was grateful for the concern and smiled at him. Simon was struck by how good looking she was. He found his eyes wandering around her body and hoped she hadn't noticed.

The Garden Centre at Sedlescombe was the largest in the area.

Although it was only just November, as soon as Simon and Louise walked through the double doors, they realised that the whole centre was lit up with newly installed Christmas decorations. One end of the large conservatory was full of decorated trees with a wide variety of white and coloured lights twinkling in different sequences. The effect was like a giant fairy grotto.

"Wow," gasped Louise.

"Happy Christmas," said Simon. "Do you like Christmas?"

"I love it, though this year might be hard without Mum." She felt tears rise in the back of her eyes. Simon put a hand on her shoulder. "It's not easy, but the pain does numb after a while." They strolled around the displays and glanced at each other, trying to appear natural. Simon found her very attractive, which increased his nervousness.

Louise changed the subject, "What is your first memory of Christmas?"

"Gosh, prehistoric times in Westfield. I guess I was about two. I remember the massive tree all lit up next to the church with carol singers on a Sunday morning. It was fun being brought up in a village. We enjoyed small pleasures. What about you? Do you remember Christmas in Singapore?"

"No, it's strange. I have no memories of Singapore, nothing at all, until I was three and I first met my grandmother on Christmas Eve in Sawbridgeworth. Apparently Mum and Dad kept me secret until they moved back to England. I've always thought that was a bit odd."

They weaved their way through the extravagant Christmas displays and admired the lights and decorations. "Do you usually have a real tree?"

"I would, if I could get it up those damn stairs at my studio!"

Simon wanted to say, "I can help you this year," but it was too soon to make plans.

Simon took charge. "How about we wander outside, while the sun is still shining, and then head to the café for a coffee?"

"Good idea." The bright November sunshine was deceptively weak, and the cold air attacked their cheeks as they walked outside to meander through the hardy shrubs. Louise began to cough. After a few minutes Simon touched one of Louise's hands. "Your hand is like ice. Let's go in."

It was 11.30 am. They ordered coffee and seated themselves in the warm atmosphere of the café. "Do you like to be called Louise or Lou?"

"I actually don't mind. My ex insisted on calling me Louise, but my mum used to call me Lou sometimes."

"Well then, Lou, how about we drive away from here and head into Sedlescombe village for lunch? There is a very good pub there."

It was decided. Simon drove very carefully as he led the way, with Louise following in her own car. They parked in the pub car park and found a seat in the small snug.

"It's one big advantage to being retired," said Simon, "The midweek pubs are not crowded at lunchtime. Shame we have to drive though, I could murder a pint."

Louise and Simon filled in the details of their family and work history over lunch. They touched on their former marriages, but each avoided too many details for fear of being perceived at fault. At 2.30 pm they walked back to their cars.

"Louise, I have really enjoyed your company. I hope we might meet again."

"I would like that very much."

He pecked her on the cheek, and they parted company.

TWELVE

Meeting Sophie

By the time Louise reached her studio, she had begun to self-doubt. 'Perhaps he was just being polite. He hasn't arranged another definite meet'.

She climbed the stairs wearily and checked the ansaphone. There were no messages.

Simon reached his house and also checked the phone. There was one message.

"Dad, Sophie has an inset day on Friday, and we forgot. Can you have her?" He rang his eldest son. "What time are you dropping her off then, Joe?"

"7.30 am. Can you do breakfast? I'll pick her up at 6 pm."

Simon had wanted to arrange a second meeting with Louise on Friday. He could, of course, ask for her help, but she might feel used. She had no children of her own, but she was a teacher. 'Did teachers actually like children?' he wondered.

Simon messaged Louise through Senior's Dating. Louise read the message straight away.

Dear Louise,

I SO much enjoyed your company today and want to see you again very soon, if you are willing.

Louise felt very positive.

Unfortunately, another woman is standing in our way.

Louise was frightened to read on.

On Friday, I have been imposed upon to mind my granddaughter, Sophie. She is a delightful child, but she is only six, so her attention span is limited. How would you feel about having lunch with me and Sophie at the Windmill in Hastings, where they have an indoor soft play area, then maybe a trip to Alexandra Park? I will pick you up if you like? Then hopefully we could plan something for just you and me at the weekend? If you haven't seen Fantastic Beasts, it is on at the Odeon.

There was lot to take in. Suddenly Louise's life had moved from empty to over-full. She only had Thursday to prepare for her outing with Simon.

Dear Simon,

Of course I will come with you and Sophie on Friday. If you pick me up, I can show Sophie (and you) my studio before we go to the Windmill. I would also very much like to watch the film with you.

Let me know what time you will come.

Louise x

Simon hoped the x was significant and regretted not signing off his own message similarly.

At 9 pm Simon noticed that Louise was connected to Senior's Dating Chat. He hoped she wasn't talking to someone else. He clicked on her name.

"Are you awake?"

"Yes, just about."

"I'm sorry about Sophie."

"It's fine. I'm looking forward to it."

"I will be at yours at about ten. I have your address."

"You can park round the back."

"I'm looking forward to it, Goodnight, Lou xx"

"Goodnight, Simon" xx

The following day she persuaded her hairdresser to fit her in again, this time to renew her highlights. She was feeling better and began to like her reflection in the salon mirror. It gave her extra confidence. She wandered into a little designer shop and bought a new top. At 9 pm a text arrived.

So looking forward to tomorrow. Sleep well, Louise xx
Night, night, Simon xx

Louise slept badly. Despite the night light, just after midnight, dreams invaded her rest. She was sitting in the dark, and Simon was holding her hand.

"You can't have him, Lou, Lou. You are mine." And Nana ripped her hand away from Simon. She woke in a sweat and began to shiver. Once again, all the lights in the flat had to be turned on.

Despite the broken night, Louise was up, dressed and ready, when Simon and Sophie knocked on the door at 10 am. Simon was once again struck by how attractive she looked.

"Sophie, how lovely to see you! Your Grandad has told me lots about you. Would you like to come inside and see where I do my painting?"

"Yes, please, Louise."

"The stairs are steep, so will you hold my hand?"

Sophie slipped her hand into Louise's grip, and they ascended together. At the top, she turned to Simon. "I told you it was steep."

"I need oxygen," he pretended to gasp.

Simon, Louise and Sophie sat at the central table for squash and biscuits. Louise put a large blank sheet of paper on one of her easels and allowed Sophie to paint colours in large swirls across the surface.

"Like a real artist," announced Louise.

"Like an amazing helper," Simon said quietly to Louise, and he slipped his arm around Louise's waist momentarily as they stood and watched the childish art.

"This place is fantastic, Lou."

"I'm pleased you like it."

Louise put Sophie's completed picture into a large plastic envelope for her to take home. The next hour was taken up with descending the stairs, settling into the car and the journey to Hastings.

"Can Louise sit in the back with me?"

"No, Sophie. Louise is mine for the journey. You have your books."

"Okay, Grandad."

They arrived at the Windmill and enjoyed a child-friendly lunch, whilst Sophie enjoyed the soft play area.

A quick walk in the park followed, and Sophie was allowed to run through the trees. Simon took Louise's hand, until Sophie ran towards them, shouting "Chase me, Grandad!" He ran after her and whisked her up into the air. "Time to go home, Sophie," he called out. With Sophie still dangling under his arm, he returned to Louise.

"I'm getting too old for this."

"It was pretty impressive," smiled Louise, and she watched, as Simon lowered Sophie to the ground, carefully securing her hand to prevent her running off. They returned to the car for the journey back to Robertsbridge. Sophie fell immediately silent in the car, and Simon soon realised she was asleep. Once in Robertsbridge, Simon turned to Louise from the driving seat and spoke quietly.

"I'm sorry, I feel really bad, but I will have to leave you here. I don't want to wake Sophie, or she'll be truly horrible. I daren't come in. Thank you so much for your help today."

"I didn't do much."

"You did masses. I will pick you up for the cinema at one thirty tomorrow. Is that okay?"

"I'm looking forward to it." Simon wanted to kiss Louise, but would not leave the car. He touched her cheek, before she got out. "I'll see you tomorrow," he whispered.

Louise was both exhilarated and exhausted. She climbed the stairs, turned on the light, then lay on her bed and fell fast asleep. When she woke at midnight, she realised she had missed a goodnight message from Simon.

The next day, she watched for his car, until he finally swung into the car park behind her flat. By the time he had rung the bell, she was half way down the stairs in her coat. She opened the door for him, and he held out a large bunch of flowers.

"To say thank you for yesterday."

Louise took the flowers and looked at the stairs. "I need to put them in water. I'll be back in a few minutes."

"I'll go. Give me your key."

And Simon shot up the stairs to put the flowers in the sink.

He returned a few minutes later. "Did you realise you've left all the lights on?"

"It will be dark, when I get back."

He placed his hand lightly against her back and led her to the car.

"No children allowed today," Simon announced as he opened the passenger door.

"She was very sweet, Simon, and very well behaved."

"Better behaved with you there."

They climbed into Simon's car. The anticipation of an afternoon alone together had increased their apprehension, and they chatted only intermittently on the twenty-minute drive to Hastings. Simon parked his car on the seafront and bought a ticket from the machine. A sharp coastal wind attacked their faces, as they left the car, and they hurried to the shelter of the town. They arrived at the cinema in plenty of time for the film. The cinema was not full, so they chose two seats in the empty third row of the raised level. Once settled, Simon took Louise's hand and twisted his fingers between hers. She felt the effect of his touch ripple through her entire body. The closeness between them was both emotional and sexually inviting. Simon was tempted to kiss her, but was aware that they were visible to the people in the seats behind. He contented himself with pressing his leg against hers. He resisted the temptation to explore her body further. Fortunately, the film was engaging despite their constant awareness of each other. They both enjoyed the fast action and compelling storyline of the movie.

They slowly adjusted their eyes to the light as they left the cinema and found Simon's car. They were very quiet on the drive home. When they reached Louise's studio, Simon got out of his car and opened the door for Louise. He pulled her into his arms, and finally kissed her for a very long time. There was no hesitation, and she was surprised by his confidence and his passion. She felt overcome by a mixture of desire and fluctuating emotions. Simon eventually broke away and spoke. "Louise, I am not coming in to your studio. I am overwhelmed with longing for you, and it is too soon. It isn't fair on you. Can I see you tomorrow?"

"Yes."

He kissed her one final time, watched her let herself in to her flat, and drove off.

THIRTEEN

Lovers

Simon arrived at 11 am the following day. Louise had left the ground floor front door unlocked, and Simon climbed the stairs to the top floor. He tapped on the inner door and entered. Louise was distracting herself with paperwork. She sat at the large central table in the studio ready to sort through one of Joan's folders. She lifted the flap and fingered the contents.

She looked up, "I'm just sorting through some papers my mother left. Oh look, it's one of my school reports from Herts and Essex High."

Simon sat down beside her.

"And what will it tell me about you?"

"It will probably say that I should concentrate more on Maths and English."

"Let me see." He took the report from her.

"You're right." He read out loud the 'Headteacher's Comments'.

"Louise would be even more successful, if she devoted as much time to her academic studies as she does to her artwork."

Simon felt the closeness of Louise's face, as they held the school report together. He lifted his hand and touched her cheek. They were both motionless, while they absorbed the moment. He brushed his finger across her mouth. She breathed deeply, stood up and walked to the studio window. The light cast shadows against her silhouette. He was once again struck by the arch of her neck and the shape of her upper body. He rose slowly, walked to the window and turned her shoulders towards him. A soft tentative kiss was followed by a more searching embrace. Their bodies pressed together as he gently manoeuvred her towards the wall of the studio. She felt the contours of his body while their mouths explored each other in excitement. He had promised himself he would not rush things, but the hunger to explore her further was beginning to consume him. She allowed him to run his hand down her back and rest his fingers under her clothing. She showed no resistance. He retrieved his hands and slowly unbuttoned the front of her blouse with care. He lifted one of her breasts from within and kissed her nipple.

Louise gasped, "You may need to take your time, Simon. It has been a very long time."

"I will treat you like a precious work of art."

He took her hand and led her towards greater intimacy. The door of the studio bedroom was closed behind them.

FOURTEEN

From Companion to Couple

The transition from companion to lover is often swift. It requires just one mutual physical act to consummate a new relationship. The journey from lover to couple takes much longer. Both Simon and Louise realised how very little they knew about each other. They had no established routines and very little shared history. Louise hadn't even visited Simon's house. Their one advantage was life experience. They had each been married before. They knew what made a relationship work and understood at least some of the pitfalls. Motivated by a mixture of strong attraction and the desire to avoid loneliness, they engaged in a silent pact to add some substance to their relationship.

Simon, especially, began to formulate a strategy. His background in computing had given him a predisposition towards forward planning. Without writing anything down, he started unconsciously to build foundations for the future.

That lunchtime when he left Louise in bed, he called out to her from the studio kitchenette, "How do you like your coffee?"

Louise appeared half dressed in the doorway.

"You charlatan. You mean you dared to have your wicked way with me without knowing how I like my coffee?"

He grinned, "There were other things about you that I needed to know more. How do you like your coffee?"

"White, strong, often."

She slipped on the rest of her clothing and came to sit in the studio. She absentmindedly put the papers from Joan back into the folder and placed them in a drawer. Simon brought over two mugs of coffee.

"I can stay until about 6 pm, but I have to go home tonight and see my son, Joe. Well I don't have to, but I think I should. After that, can I come and stay for a few days?"

Louise looked surprised.

"I want to get to know you."

Louise was pleased. "Yes of course you can. Now tell me about your house in Battle," Louise asked. "I am trying to imagine you there."

"Well maybe, when I've stayed here for a few days, you can come over to mine. That should get the neighbours talking."

"Are you overlooked?"

"Not really, but they are very nosy. Can I borrow your computer?"

He went on to google maps and showed Louise his house. It was a large, detached, grey-brick residence in a small leafy cul-de-sac. Louise was impressed.

Simon wanted to touch her, needed physical contact. He stroked her hand as they conversed.

"Now you must tell me something about you."

"There are a few things you need to know, Simon, if you are coming to stay. Most importantly, I have a recurring nightmare which wakes me up. Sometimes I scream out."

"You seem so stable. Does it go back to an event in your past?"

"It's always been a problem, ever since I was a child. Mum said it went back to a traumatic birth. I even had counselling, but it made no difference."

"How often does this happen?"

"Not normally very often, but since Mum died about twice a week, I thought I should warn you in case it happens while you're here. And I don't like the dark. It's a bit of phobia. I sleep with a night light."

"So when are the men in white coats coming?"

She smiled. "I know it is odd, but I've been like it all my life. It's not going to change now."

Simon thought about Louise being adopted. He was surprised she didn't mention it. There was surely a connection.

At 5.30 pm he made Louise a sandwich and poured her a glass of wine. "Something to remember me by."

He kissed her gently and let himself out. She watched through the window as he walked to his car.

She phoned Gillian.

"At last, my absent friend! I thought you had been kidnapped by an estate agent."

"Oh Gillian, he was not for me. He could only talk about one subject... himself, but I do have an offer of a discount if ever I sell a house."

They laughed, "Time to move on then. You mustn't give up."

"Gillian, I haven't given up. I have moved on. There's someone else."

"And you didn't tell me?"

"I needed to be sure. Now I am sure."

"You must tell me everything. How old is he? What does he do? Have you slept with him?"

"He's sixty-two, a retired website designer, and mind your own business."

"I'll take that as a yes. Sixty-two, eh? I bet he's on the Viagra!"

"I wish I hadn't told you now. Look, since you ask, people think that sex stops as you get older. But that's not true. You still want it. It just takes a bit more time and energy. Now please can we change the subject."

"Sorry. I shouldn't have mentioned it. I'm just so excited for you. When are you seeing him next?"

"He's coming to stay for a few days tomorrow."

"Blimey, I hope he likes sleeping with the lights on."

"I have told him about the lights... and about the bad dreams. He was very understanding. Gillian, this is difficult to explain, but

I think that at our age, you are more motivated to make things work, because there may not be another chance."

"You mean you are more desperate? When can I meet him?"

"Never, if you go on like this."

Gillian finally changed the subject. "How are you getting on with your mum's bungalow?"

"I've been a bit lax. Not done a thing since I met Simon. I was thinking of asking him to help me."

"Better make use of him while he's around!"

"Gillian, I have to go, he's online."

"Go ahead, desert your friend for your new man."

They finished the phone call, and Louise returned to her computer.

"*Sorry, were you busy?*" said the online message

"*I was on the phone to my friend Gillian.*"

"*Talking about me eh?*"

"*Maybe…*"

"*Is she the gay one?*"

"*Yes, you are safe from her.*"

"*I only have eyes for you. Joe said Sophie wouldn't stop talking about you.*"

"*Does he mind about me?*"

"*He just wants me to be happy. I haven't told Oliver yet though.*"

"*Will that be a problem?*"

"*Nothing that can't be sorted. I'll be with you by about 11 am. Shall I bring lunch? Then maybe we can go out for dinner. Is your local any good?*"

"*Very good, and it will give me a chance to show you off.*"

"*Oh dear, do I need to wear my best suit?*"

"*Don't be daft. Night Simon xx*"

"*Night, night Louise xx*"

Once again, the following morning, Louise watched Simon's car swing round to the back of her flat. She had left the outer door open for him. 'Should she give him a key?' she wondered. Perhaps that was a bit premature. She heard his steps on the stairs before he opened the inner door. He was carrying an overnight bag and some shopping.

"Hi, sweetheart."

Louise blushed.

"I have rolls and cold meat and salad. Is that okay?"

"Fab."

"Am I allowed to use your kitchen? Come to think of it which kitchen should I use? Your kitchen situation is very confusing."

"Even I get confused," laughed Louise "Use the downstairs one, because the dishwasher is down there, but as it's sunny, we could eat up here in the studio."

"As you wish," and Simon headed downstairs with his carrier bag of food. Louise followed.

"This is very kind, Simon."

"Pure self-interest. I am hoping for a home-cooked dinner tomorrow."

"Already planned," Louise smiled.

They carried their individual plates up to the studio and began to plan their next few days.

"We could maybe take a walk this afternoon," suggested Simon "Then dinner at the pub, and I thought we could have a day out tomorrow, before I taste your cooking. Is there anything you want to do?"

Louise decided to ask Simon a favour, "I know this is using you, but I desperately need to go to the bungalow in Fairlight and make the final arrangements for the sale. Do you think we could fit it in?"

Simon put his arm round her. "Louise, I am really sorry. I have been so excited about meeting you that I have completely ignored the fact that you have just lost your mum. Let's go together tomorrow, and then have our day out on Thursday."

"That would be brilliant."

FIFTEEN

An Intruder in Fairlight

The drive to Fairlight on the following day involved passing the entrance to the Country Park.

Simon slowed down. "Would you like to stop at the church?" asked Simon.

"Yes, please."

He parked by the teashop and let Louise take the lead. She got out of the car and looked at him, "Please hold my hand."

"I thought I might be intruding."

"I want you with me."

They walked to the grave. There was no headstone yet, just a pile of freshly-dug earth.

"I should have brought some flowers."

"We can bring them next time."

"You don't have to do this, Simon."

"I do have to do this. It was Joan who led me to you. Take your time."

Louise stood by her mother's grave for a few minutes and wiped away a tear. She turned to Simon, "Time to go."

Simon put his arm around Louise's shoulder and led her back to the car. They sat in silence until the turn to Fairlight village beckoned, and Louise was required to give directions.

"It's just up here on the right."

The small detached bungalow was located in a quiet cul-de-sac of similar bungalows. Louise got the key out of her handbag. She opened the door and entered. She noticed that the desk was once again open.

"Oh no, not again!"

"Is everything alright?" Louise told Simon about her previous suspicion of a break-in.

He shut the desk and started to jump up and down.

"Simon, what on earth are you doing?"

"I wondered if a vibration might cause it to open." He jumped again and then banged the front of the desk with the palm of his hand. "It certainly seems secure. You stay here, I'll have a look round." Simon entered the kitchen, the main bedroom and then the smaller bedroom where Louise had slept.

"Louise?"

She walked into the bedroom.

"Did you do that?"

Lying on the pillow was a large cut-out photo of Louise's face. Louise screamed.

"No, I didn't. Please believe me!"

"I believe you. Who has a key?"

"Only the neighbours."

"We need to get the locks changed."

Simon felt a moment of doubt about Louise's sanity. It occurred to him that she might have planted the photo herself, but was sure he was wrong. He rang an emergency locksmith who promised to arrive within an hour.

"Lou, you need to look round and see if anything else is different. I'll come with you."

He took her hand and noticed she was shaking. "Have a really good look."

"I can't see anything, Simon, just that bloody photo."

"Do you know when it was taken?" Louise thought for a long time, "Looking at my hair, I'd say it's about two years old. God knows where it was taken!"

The locksmith arrived swiftly and changed the locks. He gave Louise two sets of keys.

"Should I give a set to the neighbour?"

"No, I'll keep all the keys."

Louise willingly handed the new keys to Simon. "I'm going to put the cut-out photo in the desk, is that alright?"

"Yes. Will you lock up for me?" Louise began to feel sick and left the house. She took refuge in Simon's car.

"I was thinking I might come back tomorrow on my own," said Simon, "Just to check things over. You can come as well if you want."

Louise and Simon drove in silence back to Robertsbridge. He led the way upstairs and poured her a large glass of wine. He insisted that they eat their evening meal in the pub. He wanted to believe Louise was not involved in the photo incident, but was still worried she might be. He resolved to keep her in his sights and go back to the house the next day.

That night Louise woke up in terror. Nana had left her in the dark, and a tall man was carrying her towards a bright blue light. She woke Simon with a loud scream. "It's alright, Lou, it's just a dream."

She was dripping with sweat. Simon found her a towel and put on the kettle in the studio. "I'm so sorry. You must think I'm unhinged."

"Not at all," lied Simon.

The following morning he rose early. He had kept Louise in his sights ever since they left Fairlight, and he had the only keys.

"Lou, I'm going to Fairlight again. Do you want to come?" Louise hesitated, "Yes, I don't want to be left on my own."

He drove at speed to the bungalow and parked outside. He insisted that Louise stayed in the car and used the new key to open the front door. There was a draught blowing through the hallway. He stood motionless and listened, He could hear the outside wind blowing through the house. He walked back to the car, and spoke to Louise, "Something is not right. I'm sorry I doubted you."

"Did you doubt me?"

"Maybe just a little bit. I'm going to walk round the back. Lock the car behind you, hold your phone and follow me."

Simon slowly walked to the back of the bungalow. The patio door had been forced open. "Take a picture," he instructed Louise. "Are you brave enough to go in?"

"If you go first, but please be careful."

"Perhaps we should go in through the front door." Simon and Louise held hands as they walked to the front of the bungalow. He stepped into the hallway and peered into the lounge. The front of the desk was open. He pointed it out to Louise, "Look"

She turned pale. They walked to the spare bedroom and found the photo of Louise back on the pillow. "Tell me I didn't leave that photo there."

"You didn't leave that photo there."

They returned to the car, and Simon phoned the police.

"No nothing missing, just a broken patio door lock and an enlarged photo on the bed. It doesn't look like the work of kids."

Louise was as white as a sheet. "I feel really vulnerable, Simon, like someone is purposely trying to scare me."

"I think they are, Louise. There's no point in my trying to reassure you. It is scary."

Thirty minutes later, a police car arrived. The police took Simon and Louise back inside the bungalow and interviewed them. With the incident back into perspective, it began to lose some of its gravity. A cut-out photo, an open desk and a broken patio door did not cause the police undue alarm.

"Can you think of anyone who might want to frighten you?"

"I can't think of anyone."

"What about your ex-husband? Does he know about Mr Ellis?"

"I don't think he'd care if he did know. I've been divorced for almost twenty years, and he is remarried."

One of the policemen suggested again that it might be teenagers. He gave Louise a card and a crime number and instructed her not to enter the bungalow on her own. The police car sped away, and Simon secured the patio door before locking up. "Come on. Let's go home."

SIXTEEN

Different Genes

In late October and November 2016, the people of southern England were gifted an Indian Summer. Even on days when traces of windscreen frost began to emerge at dawn, clear blue skies were soon illuminated by persistent sunshine. While Simon and Louise were sitting at the table in her studio, each grasping a pre-breakfast coffee, shards of sunlight bounced off the windows and walls creating a kaleidoscope of rainbows. Simon stared around the room in admiration.

"I do understand why you love this place so much, despite the treacherous staircase. The light is amazing."

"Light like this comes with a price," explained Louise. "You need to be very high up with multi-aspect windows. Or, for a watery effect, you need to get up very early, drive to the coast, and watch the sunrise."

A voice from the Breakfast Time News interrupted their thoughts momentarily.

"The Archbishop has apologised for any 'hurt' caused by adoption agencies acting in the name of the Catholic Church. The Cardinal told a TV documentary that the practices of adoption agencies reflected the social values at that time. More than half a million adoptions took place in the thirty years before a change in the law in 1976. Many adoptions involved babies born to young unmarried mothers, and voluntary

organisations with religious affiliations often oversaw the process. Some of these young mothers have said they were pressured into giving up their babies for adoption."

"How awful to be forced to give up a baby," mused Louise, "I'm glad times have changed."

Simon put his coffee cup down. He wanted Louise to tell him more. "It must have been terrible for the young mothers who had to give up their babies, but I suppose many of the infants then grew up in loving families."

"I guess so."

"Lou? You remember at your mum's funeral that I was watching you from the tea shop?" Simon tried to sound casual.

"Stalking me, more like, a clear case of voyeurism."

Simon grinned, "I would have done, if I'd known you. Seriously, Lou, I think I told you that a man from your family came over and chatted to me briefly. He was desperate for a fag. Can you remind me who he was?"

"A bit older than me? That would be Michael, my cousin Karen's husband. Well she's not a proper cousin, second or third or once removed or something. I get confused with cousins."

"Do they live locally?"

"You're suddenly taking a lot of interest in my family."

"Well I was just thinking, if you don't get fed up with me and banish me back to Battle, I might meet him one day. It would be odd."

Once again, Louise found herself blushing. It was the first time that Simon had hinted at a long-term future together.

"I'll have to arrange a family christening." She avoided the word 'wedding', "I don't see them very often these days. Karen and Michael live in Sawbridgeworth, near Bishop's Stortford in Hertfordshire. That's the area I lived in as a child. It's a good three-hour drive from here, maybe less with you at the wheel."

Simon assumed that Louise didn't want to discuss her adoption and changed the subject.

"Shall we go down to the coast today? I promised you a day out and I hear they have staged some peculiar modern art exhibition at the De La Warr Pavillion, which I'm sure you would enjoy. We could have brunch on the seafront."

"That would be lovely."

They drove to Bexhill and parked on the seafront. The tide was out, and the persistent sunshine was reflected in the emerging sand. Louise produced a small sketchbook and sat on a bench. She traced an outline of the watery shapes, until the chill wind drove them indoors for brunch. Simon immersed himself in her company, and felt a rising sense of well-being. All his doubts about her sanity were banished by the growing closeness between them. Everything they encountered together was a new experience. He looked forward to their return to the studio and the chance to watch Louise transpose the images from her sketchbook onto the paper attached to her easel. He hoped their evening together would result in close physical contact, followed by a dream-free night. He was not disappointed.

Simon woke early the following day and left Louise in bed while he went to the local shop for bacon. On his return, he brought a letter from the lobby up to Louise. She was sitting up in bed, and he handed her an envelope with an optician's logo on the front.

"Oh, that'll be my eye test. I have to have my eyes seen annually, because my mum had glaucoma. The appointments come round ever so quickly."

Simon gave her a quizzical look. "Who did you say had glaucoma?"

"Mum, my mum, Joan Watson."

Simon tried not to look surprised. He thought quickly and responded, "It's amazing how much these medical people take account of family history."

"It's a flippin' nuisance," complained Louise.

Thoughts rushed around inside Simon's head. Michael had definitely said she was adopted. He didn't think Michael had meant it as a joke.

'If Louise is adopted, SHE DOESN'T KNOW,' His mind was working overtime in confusion. 'How can someone live for sixty-one years and not know she is adopted?'

Louise opened the fridge door. "Dammit"

"Problem?"

"I forgot to ask you to buy milk."

"We can have it black."

"No, thank you, I'll go and buy some."

"Do you want me to go?"

"I need the exercise." Louise dressed quickly, grabbed her purse and headed downstairs. Simon noticed she had left an address book by the phone. He picked it up and flicked through the pages. The name Karen jumped off the page. He looked at it and felt guilty. Then he grabbed an old receipt from his pocket and took a pencil from beside the phone. He wrote down the phone number, address, and Karen's surname. He folded the receipt and put it back in his pocket. He carefully placed the address book and pencil back in position. He instinctively moved to the other side of the studio, before Louise reappeared.

"You were quick."

"I don't waste time when I need a cup of coffee."

He tried to put his concerns to one side, before they enjoyed another day together.

SEVENTEEN

Patricia Makepiece
(1940–1955)

Patricia was clever. She was a wartime baby, conceived when her father was on leave from the airforce. Flight Lieutenant Donald Makepiece had swept Patricia's mother, Cathy, off her feet in a whirlwind pre-war romance before his impending placement brought forward their wedding to 1939. Pilot Donald Makepiece survived several airborne missions until fatally shot down in 1943. He had met his daughter, Patricia, only rarely. His widow, Cathy, was, however, well supported financially by her family and received a generous pension from the airforce, which she supplemented with sales of her watercolour paintings. Sadly, but not unusually for wartime, Cathy also lost her brother in the war and, a few years later, both her parents to pneumonia. She found herself increasingly isolated. Nevertheless, the little family consisting of only a mother and a daughter and fortnightly visits from Cathy's younger cousin, Ruby, grew in strength. Occasional men approached the mother in the hope of adding a masculine touch to the family. Cathy longed for a male companion, but could never accept an outsider being allowed to take a role in Patricia's upbringing.

Cathy filled with pride when, aged eleven, Patricia passed the scholarship for Rochester Grammar School. She took her daughter to London and paid for two full sets of uniform in navy blue. She also purchased a hockey stick and leather satchel. By the time Patricia, at fifteen, was allowed to catch the public bus from school to home on her own in the dark, after Thursday art club, she had outgrown her third adult-sized gymslip. The satchel and hockey stick were, however, still the originals.

At the end of art club, Patricia would carefully wash and dry her sable brushes before wrapping them in a cloth and placing them in the front compartment of her battered satchel. She would leave her paintings to dry in the school art room, grab her satchel and hockey stick, and run with friends to the bus stop to catch the ten past five bus. When the bus reached central Rochester, Patricia would be the only uniformed passenger left.

Her routine at the end of the final art club before the autumn half-term break was no different. Her satchel was packed with holiday homework, as she struggled to run for the bus. She still managed to clamber on board and climb the steep steps to the upper deck with her heavy load. When she alighted in Rochester, the first shimmer of Kentish night frost had appeared on the pavement. Her footsteps slowed as she carried her satchel and hockey stick across the slippery path in the churchyard to take the shortcut to her house in Penhurst Crescent. Like all the women in her family, she was tall, and looked older than her teenage years. It was only her gabardine mac and blue striped scarf which indicated her true age.

Patricia didn't hear her attacker, when he grabbed her from behind. She didn't see his face as he threw her satchel and hockey stick across the churchyard. She only felt the heat of his breath while he pinned her frame to the ground with the full weight of his body. She scarcely had time to struggle, before he had tied her scarf over her mouth and lifted her school uniform. She tried in vain to kick out as he ripped open her inner clothing. He pushed her face violently, and she momentarily heard the noise of her head knocking with force against a headstone as he thrust himself inside her. She was discovered unconscious by the church warden half an hour later. The police said the rape was both experienced and vicious. Her assailant was never found.

After two weeks of observation in hospital Patricia was

sent home into her mother's care. Cathy never spoke about the attack, but Patricia was not allowed to return to school. The GP advised three months of quiet recuperation. It was important for the scratches on her body and the swelling on her head to heal, and for Patricia to avoid questions from curious school friends. In the mid-1950s trauma was hidden and not openly discussed.

"She's young," said the doctor, "And, in time, she will no doubt forget about it."

However, by February 1955 it was obvious that Patricia was pregnant. Cathy told Patricia that the growing baby inside her was the result of the attack. It was to be kept secret. Her Auntie Ruby and the doctor were the only other people who knew. Cathy told Patricia that everything would be better once the baby was born. She bought Patricia loose fitting dresses to try and disguise her condition, but, as she grew nearer to full term, Patricia was hidden from view. Neighbours assumed that the teenager was still recovering from her attack, and plans were put in hand to confine Patricia in a convent in nearby Chatham for her final month. The baby would be adopted, and Patricia would be allowed to resit her school year from the following September. No other option for the baby's future care was ever considered. Despite her daughter's status as a victim, Cathy felt the full shame of Patricia's situation.

In the early summer of 1955 Patricia was sent to the convent. Cathy tried not to imagine her daughter's fear as the nuns supervised her labour. She wondered if Patricia would be allowed to hold her baby before the infant was whisked away to a nursery full of illegitimates. She knew that the nuns did not place a high value on the needs of their under-age mothers. She realised that her daughter's rape would not result in any special treatment. Nevertheless, Cathy was overcome with shock when, two days later, the convent telephoned to inform Cathy that Patricia had died very suddenly from unexplained causes. They told Cathy that the attending doctor had suspected a brain clot caused by Patricia's prior head injury, but the death certificate gave the cause of death as 'childbirth'.

Cathy caught the bus to the convent and demanded to see the baby.

"This is a most unusual request, Mrs Makepiece. The child is already booked out for adoption. We will be asking you to sign the papers today."

"The child is my next of kin. I have a right to see her."

And the sister nodded to a junior nun who left the reception room and returned a few minutes later with a tiny infant tightly wrapped in a lace shawl. She placed the baby girl on Cathy's lap. Cathy stroked the child's cheek and placed her finger in the miniature hand. She watched the baby's eyes as they tried to focus on her grandmother's face. A likeness to Patricia was already evident, and Cathy's overwhelming grief at the loss of her daughter lifted when she looked at her granddaughter.

The two nuns exchanged glances. "The child has bad blood. She is the issue of a violent conception. She will need a very strict upbringing to help her to avoid the evil within her. We have found a suitable couple to take on the task."

"The child is my granddaughter. I am taking her home."

EIGHTEEN

Nana

Cathy signed the release papers and emerged through the heavy wooden door of the convent with the baby in her arms. Once the sisters had seen the strength of Cathy's resolve, they made no objection.

Cathy held the tiny baby close, as she waited at the bus stop. The infant was beginning to turn her lips towards Cathy's breast, and she hoped that the crying would wait until they reached Penhurst Crescent. Seemingly unused to bodily contact, the baby felt a new contentment in the heat of her grandmother's body and chose not to cry. Once back on home territory, Cathy bought powdered milk, bottles, rubber teats and nappies on the walk back to their house in Penhurst Crescent. She laid the lace-wrapped baby in an empty drawer and boiled a saucepan of water in which to warm the milk. Sterilising the bottle would have to wait. Once separated from her grandmother, the child began to shriek.

However, within five minutes the tiny child was purring with delight as she drew milk from the bottle into her mouth. For several days, Cathy and the baby remained incarcerated in isolation together. Cathy boiled the nappies daily and dried them in front of the gas fire. She cut up old pillow cases and sheets for bedding and spare clothes. She bathed the baby every evening and found some vaseline to smooth on her granddaughter's skin. Eventually, she realised she would need to venture outside. How on earth would Cathy explain her new arrival to the neighbours, her family, the vicar? No one, except Cathy, the doctor and her cousin, Ruby, knew that Patricia had been pregnant. "Let them wonder," said Cathy out loud. "I will say nothing. They will think the child is mine. I will call her Louise. It was Patricia's middle name."

A week after baby Louise was installed in the family home in Rochester, Cathy's neighbours watched Ruby arrive pushing a brand new pram filled with parcels to the front door of Cathy's Victorian house. Two hours later, the two cousins emerged from the house dressed in black and climbed into a taxi with babe in arms.

"That accounts for the closed curtains," said a neighbour to her friend. There has been a bereavement. Patricia's funeral had been speedily held by the nuns, even before Cathy had been informed of her daughter's death. Patricia had been assigned no more privileges than any other young unmarried mother. She had been buried in a distant corner of the convent grounds which was reserved for the purpose. Cathy had nevertheless insisted on visiting the grave with Ruby and Louise. She wanted somewhere to take Louise regularly to be close to her mother's resting place. It was made very clear by the nuns, however, that Cathy would not be a welcome visitor. This one and only entry to the convent grounds would be allowed for reflection and prayer. They led the cousins to Patricia's resting place. The small stone heading was engraved with the two words 'Patricia Makepiece'. Ruby held the baby as Cathy knelt by the grave. She then passed the child to her grandmother, and Ruby lowered herself towards the ground. She took a sharp penknife from her bag and secretly scratched a kiss as deeply as she could on the back of the stone. Tears rolled down her cheeks as the Sister of Mercy led them both out of the convent grounds and said they could not visit again.

"We must not be seen to condone evil, Mrs Makepiece."

Cathy had always been reasonably close to her neighbours. The post-war community of spacious, privately-owned, and prestigious terraced houses was filled with ex-officers and their wives who understood each other's backgrounds. Cathy was the only widow amongst them and tended to be regarded as slightly unusual due to her lack of interest in remarriage and her obsession with painting. Nevertheless, she had still chatted with other mothers at the school gate and been called upon to use her artistic flair to decorate cakes for birthday parties. When Patricia was withdrawn from school in 1954, neighbours simply assumed that Patricia was unwell from the attack. They brought gifts of flowers and home-made soup. However, they soon noticed that Cathy had changed. After the attack, she appeared cold and did not invite them into the house. The neighbours eventually stopped calling.

Now, unexpectedly, there had been a funeral. Patricia had disappeared, and in her place was a pram filled with child. Cathy's situation was a cause of continual whispered conversations and twitching curtains. The neighbours suspected that Ruby might not have been virtuous, and Cathy was covering up for her transgression.

A week after Cathy visited the grave, the newly-appointed local vicar paid a call. He was invited in and offered tea and home-made cake. Cathy had never held religious figures in high esteem, but her encounter with the nuns had made her even more wary. She was determined to keep her secret.

"I am told you have been recently bereaved, Mrs Makepiece."

"Sadly, yes, my daughter, Patricia, died of tuberculosis."

"The funeral was not local?"

"Patricia was kept in isolation because of the risk of contagion. She was in the care of the Sisters of Mercy who arranged her funeral."

"My sincere condolences, Mrs Makepiece." The vicar was new to the area and assumed that Cathy was Catholic. He had no reason to disbelieve her story. He walked over to the pram and regarded the sleeping baby. "She is beautiful, Mrs Makepiece. What is her name?"

"Louise, my daughter's name is Louise."

"Such a pretty name. Your husband must be so proud."

"I'm afraid I am a widow."

The vicar assumed that her husband had also died recently.

"You have had such a sad time, Mrs Makepiece. I will remember you in my prayers."

Cathy smiled at her unintended deception, as the vicar left the house. The neighbours would, of course, notice that little Louise called her 'mother' by the name of "Nana". Indeed, they did often discuss the child's possible history behind Cathy's back, but they did not share their many suspicions with the vicar. He was unmarried, so there was no vicar's wife to take on one side and infect with whispered gossip.

NINETEEN

Losing Louise

Cathy was besotted with her granddaughter. With no husband to care for, and no allowances made by anyone, except Ruby, for her grief at the loss of her own daughter, Patricia, she clung to the baby for comfort. All her excess widow's pension and all her energy was spent on her granddaughter. She ignored the current fashion of providing a pink and floral environment for a girl-child and painted the walls of one of her spare bedrooms, now a nursery, with farm animals, rainbows, and brightly coloured letters of the alphabet. She sang songs, read stories and watched with pleasure as Louise began to take notice. She took the pram to the park and chatted to the anonymous gatherings of young mothers. She soon realised that her Louise seemed advanced in comparison to most other babies and toddlers of a similar age. Louise walked at eleven months and was talking clearly in complex sentences before the age of two. Cathy showed two-year old Louise how to dip a paintbrush into a pot of brightly coloured paint and make lines on large sheets of paper. She taught the child how to push large stubby crayons in semi circles and create the very same rainbows, which Louise loved to see on the nursery wall. Cathy refused to employ a full-time nanny in her home for Louise, but she did employ a retired housekeeper, Mrs Phelps, who visited twice weekly to clean the kitchen, lounge and nursery. Mrs Phelps also adored Louise and allowed the toddler to help dust the tables and sweep the floor with her toy dustpan and brush. She patiently accepted the accidents, as Cathy began to teach Louise to go without nappies. By the age of two, Louise was completely dry. Cathy's younger cousin, Ruby, visited often. She was several years junior to Cathy and still living with her own parents in South London. Being the oldest of seven children, Ruby was more than willing to escape to the quieter environment and 1950's affluence of the house in Rochester. She understood children and their development, and was happy to help with Louise. She also felt privileged that Cathy had chosen to tell her Patricia's secret, even before Louise had been born.

"It's amazing that Lou Lou is so confident with other adults, Auntie Cathy." The childhood title of Auntie was still used. "I mean she doesn't see a lot of different adults, does she?"

"That child is loved," interrupted Mrs Phelps, "Loved in every ounce of her little body. And them's that's loved, give love back, don't they, little Louise?"

Mrs Phelps lifted Louise up to her own eye level. "Say, 'I love Nana'."

"I love Nana," repeated Louise, and she blew an extravagant kiss towards Cathy as she had been taught by Mrs Phelps. The room erupted into laughter. There was no strict regime of fashionable rules in Louise's early upbringing. She was reared with a combination of common sense discipline and unwavering love which gave the child both self-confidence and security. Louise's natural affability was nurtured and rewarded. She was praised for giving affection and being kind to others. Subject to the inevitable self-centredness of a two-year old, Louise began to develop into an outward-looking and well-balanced human being.

When Louise was two and a half, Cathy began to get frequent headaches. "I can hardly bear them," she told her doctor, "and I keep forgetting things."

"What things?"

"Shopping, peoples' names, the ends of my sentences."

"We all do that, Mrs Makepiece, and it is tiring bringing up a child on your own. Louise has no father to help with discipline. Are you coping?"

"Yes of course," replied Cathy in irritation. She resented the idea that a man was needed in a house to enforce discipline. She resolved not to visit her doctor again. She would buy herself some more aspirin for her headaches.

Ruby also began to notice her older cousin's forgetfulness and resolved to visit more often. On one such visit, Cathy went out to the shops and confessed to Ruby that she had forgotten her way home. She had to ask for directions.

"You really should go back to the doctor's, Aunty Cathy."

"I will, if it happens again," Cathy lied.

Ruby was worried about her cousin, and decided to offer to come and stay for a month in early August as a belated celebration of Louise's third birthday. She returned back home to South London to pack a larger bag and bring back some presents for Louise.

It was late July 1958, two days after Louise's third birthday. Mrs Phelps had taken a week's leave, and Cathy and Louise were alone in the house. Just before teatime, Cathy realised there was no bread in the pantry. She walked out of the house to go shopping and forgot to take Louise with her. She wandered to the end of her road and wondered where she was. She saw a park in the distance, which looked familiar, and walked towards the large green space. Cathy sat down on a bench in the park to think. Eventually, darkness descended. The silhouettes of the trees began to send shadows across the grass.

Louise had been playing at home in the nursery. Now feeling hungry, she slowly descended the stairs and called out for her Nana. There was no reply. She checked every room. Nana could not be found. It was getting darker, and Louise climbed on a chair to turn on the light switch. She walked into the kitchen and opened a cupboard. She found a packet of biscuits and placed it on the kitchen table. She found her cup, climbed on to her little step and carefully filled the cup with water from the tap. She sat at the table in the front room with the biscuits and the water. Two hours later, the electric meter ran out of money, and the house was plunged into darkness. Louise screamed out for Nana. She tried to move around but kept walking into furniture. She wondered if there were monsters approaching her through the blackness. She grabbed a cushion and hugged it for comfort. Eventually she lay on the floor and sobbed herself to sleep.

Cathy sat on the bench in the park for several hours. She was discovered at 9.30 pm by the park keeper, as he checked for last-minute visitors before locking up. He noticed a smartly dressed lady sitting motionless on a distant bench. He approached cautiously.

"You alright, Missus?"

Cathy looked at the park keeper, "Of course, I'm alright."

"Well shouldn't you be on your way home? I need to lock up, and it's getting cold."

"Home, yes I need to go home."

Cathy stood up and started to walk further into the park. The park keeper followed her and turned her round. "You're going the wrong way. This is the way out."

He led Cathy through the park gates and directed her to an external seat. He locked the gates and watched her from a distance. Eventually he returned to the bench.

"Are you unwell? Can I ring someone for you? I could get you a taxi."

Cathy just stared into space.

"Where do you live, love? I can't just leave you here."

"I live with Louise."

"Shall I call Louise, then? Do you have the number?"

"Louise is not allowed to answer the telephone."

The park keeper sat down beside her, unsure what to do. His office would be closed by now, and he didn't know who to turn to.

"Look, love, I'm going to try and find someone to help you. You stay sitting on this bench."

He walked to a nearby telephone box and dialled 999.

"Emergency Services. Which service do you require?"

"Well I'm not really sure. I'm the park keeper at Rochester Gardens. There's this woman, nicely dressed, about my age, and she's just staring into space. She won't move."

"Is she ill? Or drunk?"

"I don't think so. She was talking to me, posh voice. She said she lived with someone called Louise, but she wouldn't tell me where. I think she might have had a bang on the head. She seems to have forgotten her address."

"Have you looked in her handbag for an address? I presume she has a handbag?"

"Yes, she's gripping it tightly. I didn't like to try and go through it."

"I'll send a police constable in a car. Can you stay with her until he arrives?"

"The wife will be worried, but of course I'll stay."

The police car arrived fifteen minutes later, and a uniformed constable got out and sat next to Cathy.

"Are you alright love? Have you had a fall?"

"No, I don't think so."

"What's your name?"

"Cathy, Cathy Makepiece"

"It's cold out here and dark. Do you live in Rochester?"

"Rochester, yes, I live in Rochester."

"Can you tell me your address?"

"Oh, I'll think of it in a minute. It's just slipped my mind."

"Let's have a look in your handbag, shall we?"

The constable took her bag and opened the catch. He found a post office savings book with an address on the inside cover.

9, Penhurst Crescent, Rochester, Kent.

"That's a nice part of town. Climb in my car, and I'll run you home. The park keeper said you live with a lady called Louise. Is that right?"

"It's dark. Louise will be in bed."

The policeman drove the five-minute journey to Cathy's house.

"You stay in the car, love. I'll go and knock on the door."

It was dark, and there was no reply. He turned on his torch and peered through the patterned stained glass in the front door. The house appeared to be empty. He noticed the front room curtains were open. He shone his torch through the net curtain. He caught a glimpse of what looked like a young child lying on the floor.

He hurried back to the car. "Cathy, how old is Louise?"

"She's three."

"Stay in the car."

The policeman smashed the glass on the front door with his truncheon and turned the inside latch. He shone his torch into the front room and saw the child asleep on the floor. Thankfully she was breathing.

Cathy recognised her own home, climbed out of the car, and walked into her house. She instinctively opened the hall cupboard door, emptied the money jar on the shelf and fed the electricity meter. The house lit up. Louise woke with a start.

"Nana!"

Cathy cuddled her granddaughter. "You should be in bed. It's late!"

The constable used the house phone to call for help, while Cathy hugged the sobbing child. Within half an hour two more uniformed officers arrived, followed by an ambulance.

"Cathy, we are going to look after Louise for you tonight. You have to give her to us."

Cathy held onto Louise and refused to let her go.

"I wouldn't let the nuns have her, and you're not having her either!" Cathy shouted aggressively at the policeman. The ambulance driver began to untangle Louise's fingers from her grandmother's clothing. He managed to take hold of the girl, and handed her to one of the policemen. The hysterical screaming child was held tightly in the back of the car, while his companion drove directly to the child welfare centre in Chatham. Back in the house, Cathy began to lash out with her limbs. She tried to kick the remaining policeman. "You can't steal my Louise! She's mine."

It took two strong men to pin Cathy down and strap her into a straight-jacket. Eventually, the ambulance delivered the young grandmother to Rochester General Hospital. A policeman was despatched to Mrs Phelps' address, which had been found in Cathy's address book.

When Mrs Phelps visited Rochester General the following day, Cathy was heavily sedated and unable to communicate. Mrs Phelps gave the ward sister contact details for Ruby and left the hospital knowing that she had probably lost contact forever with a charming and unusual child, not to mention a lucrative part-time job.

Ruby met with child welfare three days later at Cathy's house. She was asked if her own family could take Louise in. Ruby explained that she was the oldest of seven. Taking in another child would not be possible.

Ruby asked if she could visit Louise. This, said Child Welfare, was not advisable. Louise would most likely be adopted and needed to forget her past. At three years old, Louise was young enough to make a fresh start with a new family. Ruby showed the official into Louise's nursery and packed a small suitcase with her most precious items, a few clothes, paintings, paper and crayons, her favourite doll, and a photo of Nana outside the house in Penhurst Crescent. Ruby hurriedly wrote the word Nana on the back of the photo. She tucked it into a side pocket of the case. The official drove away from the house leaving Ruby to deal with the legal implications of an empty house and a grandmother taken into care.

TWENTY

Adoption

The end of the Second World War in 1945 presented unexpected problems for employment. Whilst there were plenty of jobs for the lower military ranks, who were generally physically fit with much needed skills in basic engineering, building and manual labour, career opportunities for commissioned officers were less plentiful. Many had grown accustomed to the privileges of their rank, and they had inflated expectations of their potential income. Most wanted to stay in the forces, but were not allowed to do so. Peter Watson was one of the more fortunate ex-officers. As the eldest son of a high-ranking diplomat, he had spent his childhood in Singapore and had acquired a basic fluency in Malay. In 1946 he was offered a placement in Singapore, as an executive officer in the Diplomatic Service. He was part of the British team which supported Singapore's transition to a Crown Colony. He travelled out to the Far East, aged just twenty-six years old, and was placed in the care of the local Assistant Secretary. Trips back to the UK were allowed annually to visit family and meet up with Civil Service colleagues. On his UK visit in 1948 he met a pretty eighteen-year old shorthand typist, named Joan, at the foreign office. Joan was petite with curved, rounded hips, which Peter found very attractive. Joan and Peter began to correspond, when he returned to Singapore, and he later wrote to Joan's father to ask for her hand in marriage, requiring her parent's consent, as she was then under-age. Joan's parents were well aware of the benefits to their daughter of such a match and readily agreed. Peter obtained special leave to return to England for his wedding and took his new young wife, now aged nineteen, back to Singapore where they set up home together until the Spring of 1958. Having lived on her parents' Essex farming estate all her life, Joan was accustomed to a combination of affluence and physical hard work. She easily adjusted to the heat and social demands placed upon an expat wife. She enjoyed entertaining, and her upper-middle-class accent fitted well in diplomatic circles. Learning to manage a household of Malaysian servants was more of a challenge, but, with Peter's support, she soon learnt to run her new home with a mixture of authority and kindness. She missed England, rarely saw her parents, but enjoyed her new life. Lack of children was her one real regret. Despite a loving relationship with her husband, the babies never happened.

When Peter was informed about the closure of his section in Singapore, he was offered a senior post in the Foreign Office in Whitehall. Joan and Peter decided to return to the UK and to adopt a baby. They would aim to live within commuting distance of central London, but in a reasonably rural setting as close as possible to Joan's parents. They rented a house in the little town of Sawbridgeworth in Hertfordshire. Joan had visited the town because she had a cousin who lived there. If they settled, the couple decided that they would purchase a property as soon as possible. Joan was excited at the prospect of finally owning their own house and embarked on a property search with enthusiasm. She understood Peter's traditional taste, and soon found a large well-appointed detached Edwardian house with many original features. Subject to agreed guidelines, Peter was more than happy to leave domestic arrangements to his wife. He readily agreed to her choice of property, and the purchase was rapidly completed.

Joan and Peter had applied by letter from Singapore to adopt a baby when their return to the UK was imminent. Joan was now twenty-eight, and they had been trying for a family for seven years without success. Peter was ten years older than Joan, and they didn't want to wait any longer. In the 1950s there was a ready supply of parentless babies seeking new homes. The screening procedure for potential adopters was uncomplicated. Most childless couples were approved, as long as they had an income, home and no criminal record. Generally speaking, babies would be allocated to parents 'out of area' to protect the biological mothers from an accidental encounter with their child.

Joan had requested a girl, and had indicated her willingness to take a child up to the age of three years, though, in her imagination, she always assumed that she would be given a baby. Once back in England, Joan resisted the temptation to buy baby clothes, but she and Peter employed a decorator to wallpaper one of the spare bedrooms in their newly-purchased house with patterned rosebuds in anticipation of their possible new arrival. When the phone call came, it was an invitation to visit a children's home in Kent.

"The child is just three years old, bright, pretty and from a loving middle-class home. She is already potty trained, speaks clearly and likes drawing pictures. We are not allowed to give you any background details, but we would like to place her as a matter of urgency."

Peter took a day's leave, and the couple drove to Chatham.

Peter filled his car with petrol just South of the Blackwall Tunnel and then steered his Austin Cambridge through the more rural roads south of the river. Joan had the Ordnance Survey map on her lap and would occasionally issue instructions.

"Left here, after the pub."

"Look for a sign to Rochester."

"Less than three miles now, it might be signposted."

And sure enough, two miles later, a small white sign with black writing indicated the turning to Hellingham House. Peter stretched out his right arm and signalled left through the open window. He turned the steering wheel sharply. The children's home was approached via a lengthy, tree-lined gravel drive. The impressive entrance, however, did not disguise the rotting wooden window ledges and badly-pointed brickwork. Peter parked his car under a tree, and the couple walked to the front door. Joan heard children's voices and felt a flutter of excitement. A smart middle-aged woman opened the door.

"Mr and Mrs Watson, my name is Mary Clancy, and I work for the Kent Child Welfare Service. Welcome."

She led the couple into a comfortable lounge with leather chairs. A box of toys was discreetly tucked in a corner. Once seated, a pot of tea was placed before them. Mrs Clancy spoke as she poured the tea.

"Louise is an unusual case."

'Louise,' thought Joan, 'She has a name. Her name is Louise.'

Mary Clancy continued, "Unlike many of our older placements, Louise has been well nurtured in a caring and disciplined home environment. She comes from a middle-class, educated home background and should fit easily into your family. Her last few weeks before joining us were troubled, but will soon be forgotten. I am not authorised to share any more with you. If you decide to take her on, then I strongly recommend that you do not tell her she is adopted. Some questions are better not to be asked."

Mrs Clancy rang the bell, and an older girl with plaited hair and a white apron appeared.

"Sheila, can you please ask Matron to send Louise down?"

Sheila left, and Mary Clancy explained, "We like to give some responsibility to our older girls."

A few minutes later the lounge door opened, and a woman in nurse's uniform stood in the doorway. Holding her hand was a small blonde-haired child in a waisted frock with embroidered bodice. Her hair had been plaited with pink ribbons tied at each end.

"Louise, say hello to Mrs Watson."

Joan rose to her feet and approached the child. She then dropped to her knees to achieve face-to-face contact. She touched one of Louise's pink ribbons.

"You have such pretty hair. Do you like pink ribbons?"

"My favourite colour is purple, but I quite like pink."

Joan was taken aback by Louise's confident response.

"You know your colours then," Joan thought quickly, "I have a bedroom at home with pink flowers on the wall. I am hoping that one day a little girl like you will come and stay there."

"I like drawing flowers," responded Louise. "Can I draw you some flowers?"

Matron produced some paper and crayons and sat Louise down at a little table. Louise carefully selected the different colours and produced an image of green stems and purple petals.

"That's a beautiful picture, Louise, may I keep it?"

"It's for you. I will draw another one later for Nana."

Joan glanced at Matron, "Are you sure she is only just three?"

"She is tall for her age, and bright, but, yes, we are sure. We have her birth certificate."

Peter stood up and walked towards the child. Louise left the table and clung to Matron's legs.

"Louise's experience of men is somewhat limited, I'm afraid. And her last encounter with a man was with the police constable who brought her here." Joan dared not ask for details. Instead she enticed Louise back out by looking at one of the toys in the box. After fifteen minutes of play, Louise was taken away by matron for her tea.

Mary Clancy spoke frankly to Joan and Peter.

"Louise should not be here. She is a stable, talented child who will benefit from a loving home. I am going to leave you alone with your husband for a short while. When I return, I will offer Louise to you for a six week stay, at the end of which we will suggest that you make a donation to Hellingham House. We will then sign the adoption papers."

"What will you tell Louise?"

"That she is going on holiday to stay in the room with pink rosebuds. Young children have very short memories, Mrs Watson. Louise will soon forget she was ever here."

Mary Clancy left Peter and Joan alone. Joan felt her eyes fill with tears.

"Why so emotional?" asked Peter. "Tell me what you are thinking."

"I can't believe that they are giving us this delightful child."

"Possibly not 'giving', a donation was mentioned," grinned Peter.

"And we can take her today? I'll have to sit in the back with her. We will need the travel blanket to keep her warm. I don't have anything suitable for tea. Did we make up the little bed?"

"I take it you want her," said Peter.

Joan's eyes welled up, "I want her so much."

As if she had been listening, Mary Clancy re-entered the room.

"Have you made a decision?"

"We'll take her. Will she be afraid of the car?" asked Peter.

"She'll probably sleep, but, if not, I suggest you stop on the way back for a snack. She likes her food."

Louise appeared fifteen minutes later in her woollen tailored coat carrying a doll and a small suitcase. Joan pulled out Louise's recently crayoned picture of the flowers from her bag.

"I am going to pin this on the wall of the bedroom with the pink roses, but I am not sure where exactly to put it. Matron has said you can come home with us to help us decide, and then stay for a holiday."

Peter looked fondly at his wife. He was astounded at how good she was with the child. They left Hellingham House as a family of three. Peter quickly took a few photos, then Louise took Joan's hand, and they walked to the car together.

TWENTY-ONE

Meeting Grandma

Joan's family was small, but close knit. Her father and uncle were farmers who owned a large estate in northern Essex about an hour's journey from Sawbridgeworth, where Joan and Peter had recently bought their house. Only one cousin lived nearby. Once little Louise had fallen asleep on the polished leather seat in the back of the Austin Cambridge, Peter and Joan began to discuss how to keep Louise's adoption a secret.

"I don't see how we can do it," said Joan. "They'll all want to visit, and they'll gush all over her with kisses and cuddles. The word 'adoption' is bound to be heard by Louise."

"Then we won't tell them," announced Peter, "Though I think we can trust Karen. She'll understand."

"True, but what about my parents?"

"And Uncle Jack," added Peter.

"Oh, god, I'd forgotten about Uncle Jack," Joan covered her face in mock horror.

"How important is it that Louise never knows about her adoption?" questioned Peter.

"Mary Clancy said it was very important. I wish she had given us more information about Louise though."

"Sometimes things are best left in the past, Joan. How long have we got, before your parents visit?"

"I'd guess, we have until Christmas."

Peter was used to being in charge. He saw his role as the solver of family problems. "Let me think about this, Joan."

It was dark by the time their car drove up to their house in Sawbridgeworth. Peter unlocked the front door and switched on the hall light. He climbed the stairs and moved a bedside light into Louise's bedroom. Joan lifted the sleeping child from the back of the car and carried her upstairs. She removed Louise's coat and shoes and tucked her under the sheets and blankets.

"We'd better leave the small light on," Peter whispered.

Peter and Joan stood in the bedroom doorway and watched the little body moving gently with each breath under the bedclothes. Peter put his arm around Joan, and she felt a rogue tear trickle down her cheek. Peter produced a white handkerchief and wiped his wife's face.

By the time Joan's parents were invited to stay in Sawbridgeworth, Peter and Joan had agreed a detailed story to explain Louise's history. They rehearsed it so often that they almost began to believe it themselves. Peter's severance payment from the Diplomatic Service had funded the purchase of their new home, and his salary in his senior civil service post had ensured a comfortable future for them both. Uncle Jack had agreed to look after the farm, so Joan's parents could visit the house and stay in luxury for three nights over Christmas. Joan had insisted they come early and told them she had a surprise for them. Her parents assumed that the surprise would be a tour of the new property.

Joan watched nervously for the Land Rover to pull into the drive. Peter stood beside his wife to give her support. This would be the first meeting between daughter and parents, since Joan and Peter had returned to the UK. The vehicle arrived. Heavy car doors swung open, and Lillian and Jim climbed out. Jim pulled back the cover and revealed boxes of fresh vegetables together with bags of wrapped gifts. As soon as he saw Joan, he put the presents down and hugged her, until firmly pushed aside by his wife. He shook hands with Peter, who then helped with the boxes, and the family group entered the house. Coats were hung up, and they all moved into the spacious living room.

"Well, this is a fine-looking property, Peter."

There was no time to waste. A little person was being kept hidden by her Auntie Karen upstairs, but would not be quiet for long.

"Mummy, Daddy, we have something to tell you. Please sit down."

Lilly and Jim sensed the urgency and felt a moment of concern. They sat as directed.

"Look, we're sorry we didn't tell you before, but we couldn't get permission to bring her home and show you."

"What on earth are you trying to tell us?" asked Jim. "Have you brought a dog back from Singapore?"

Peter laughed out loud, "It's my fault. I wanted it to be a surprise. I'm just going to have to say it, "We have a daughter, your granddaughter. Her name is Louise."

He had silenced the entire room.

Karen tapped on the living room door. "Can we come in?"

"Yes," gasped Joan.

Karen led the wide-eyed three year old into the room. Her blonde hair had been tied into curly pigtails with purple ribbons. She was wearing a matching smocked velvet dress with white ankle socks and shiny patent shoes. "Remember what I taught you, Louise," instructed Karen.

Louise walked slowly towards Lillian.

"Hello, Grandma."

Lillian burst into tears, and Louise retreated back to the safety of her Auntie Karen.

"Are you alright, Mummy?" asked Joan, "I'm sorry, I didn't mean to upset you."

"Upset, me? Of course I'm upset. Jim, we have to go out now!"

"But we've only just arrived," protested Jim.

"We're going into Bishops Stortford. What time do the shops shut?"

"Probably late afternoon on Christmas Eve. Why on earth are we going shopping?"

"This is my first Christmas with my granddaughter," sobbed Lillian. "She must have a present from her grandma!"

Everybody laughed. "I'll drive," insisted Peter.

"And I'll bring the cheque book," said Jim with a resigned smile.

They departed almost immediately, leaving Joan, Karen and Louise in the house to recover their sanity.

Lillian brought so many presents that Peter could barely fit them all in the back of his car. Her favourite toy was a large farm on a folding board with little velvet bags of wooden animals. She hoped that Joan would allow Louise to come and stay on the farm soon, and wanted to prepare the child.

Louise woke at 7 am on Christmas morning, and the entire family gathered in the living room to watch the little girl unwrap her presents. Each adult took it in turns to fold the discarded paper. Jim remarked how one little blonde child had the power to unite a family in never-before-seen ways. He was at first worried that the group adoration of Louise would result in a lack of discipline, but soon realised that Joan had a natural no-nonsense approach with the child, which combined with Peter's traditional notion of right and wrong would ensure a sensible upbringing. He would leave it to Lillian to offer unlimited indulgence.

Karen had returned to her own family for Christmas Day, and, once the presents were opened, Joan took Louise upstairs for a rest. Lillian followed to watch the routine. Joan tucked Louise up in her bed and said she would return in an hour. The curtains were left open.

"You've forgotten to close the curtains," observed Lillian. "Oh, I don't bother," Joan told her mother. Louise settles better in the light. It took her quite a while to adjust to the new time zone, when we moved from Singapore." Joan had created such a credible story about Louise's birth, that she had become skilled at answering unexpected queries.

"Apart from the occasional nightmare, she sleeps really well."

116

"Nightmares are a sign of a good imagination," Lillian said.

Louise slept while the adults drank milky coffee. Joan had boiled the milk and filled the silver coffee set which she had brought back from Singapore. There was a ring on the door. A ten-year-old boy stood on the doorstep holding a small wrapped gift. "Happy Christmas, Mrs Watson, I have bought a present for Louise."

"She's asleep, Bob, but you can wait until she wakes, if you like. Come and meet my parents." Joan lowered her voice, "Don't forget the secret."

"I won't."

Joan introduced Bob, and with Joan's permission, Bob sat on the carpet and set out the little farm animals in anticipation of Louise's reappearance. Joan suspected there were more toys for him in her house, than in his own home. At exactly midday, Louise's voice was heard.

"Mummy," Joan still felt emotional when she heard that word.

"Coming, darling."

Joan climbed the stairs to Louise's bedroom. Louise was sitting up.

"Bob's here."

"Bob Bob."

Mother and daughter slowly negotiated the stairs. Louise stared at the farm and shouted, "Manimals!"

Everybody laughed. Louise walked up to her mother and said, "Paper, Mummy... please and crayons."

"You can use your new easel, Louise."

Joan erected the little artist's easel, which she had brought Louise for Christmas. Louise smiled, "Like Nana's."

"She has a pretend friend," Joan explained to her own mother.

Joan handed a box of fat colourful crayons to Louise. Her little fingers pulled out a purple crayon, and she carefully drew the outline of a large pig. She turned the crayon on its side and shaded the centre of the pig.

"Purple pig," she announced, "For grandma's farm."

She carefully pulled the top sheet of paper away from the easel. She carried the picture to give to Lillian, then sat on the floor with Bob and played with the animals. Lillian scrutinised the picture.

"An artist! You have given birth to an artist! This is really good for her age. You only produced scribble when you were three. Where does she get it from? Are there artists in your family, Peter?"

"Not that I know of Lillian. Can you draw, Jim?"

"No, but I can mend a tractor. Louise needs to learn to do something useful."

Louise picked up the toy tractor from her farm set. "Tractor," she said, and everybody laughed.

TWENTY-TWO

Bob

History has largely ignored the plight of post-war military babies. Many couples rushed into marriage and started families in the euphoria of sudden peacetime. Consequently, babies were born to mothers who barely knew their new husbands. Robert Cornelius Gresham was one such child. Born in February 1946, he was the product of an impetuous post-war marriage between a recently-discharged, non-commissioned, soldier and a land girl. They struggled to make a living and to strengthen the shaky foundations of their relationship. When Robert's father was finally offered a job as a mechanic at a riverside workshop in Sawbridgeworth, Hertfordshire, the family welcomed the chance of a fresh start. They managed to rent a reasonably spacious first-floor flat on the outskirts of town close to a prestigious more affluent area. Robert, known as Bob, was registered at the local primary school, and the family found some much-needed stability. Bob showed an aptitude for arithmetic, and settled into his new class. He was much loved by his pretty blonde mother, who soon fell pregnant again. The family looked forward to expanding their numbers. Sadly, however, Bob's mother died in childbirth with a still-born child when Robert was seven. Bob's father soon remarried, and Bob's care was transferred to his father's new, younger, wife, an equally pretty, but far less caring, twenty year old. Bob quickly learned to take second place to his stepmother's needs, and later to those of his new baby brother. However hard he tried to please his stepmother, he was constantly criticised, and he felt overwhelmed with failure. Despite his continued success in lessons, he began to try too hard to make friends. The more popular boys bullied him, and the girls sneered behind his back. He became a lonely figure on the school playground.

His greatest supporter was a distant neighbour, Joan. Shortly after Joan moved to Sawbridgeworth, and before Louise was adopted, she noticed the solitary boy wandering through the nearby streets and engaged him in conversation. Coming from an expat background where more affluent families were expected to take an interest in the affairs of their less fortunate neighbours, this seemed the natural thing to do. Joan and her husband invested time in Robert, and when Louise arrived, Bob was often included in tea parties and outings. He became devoted to Louise. He adored her blonde hair and gentle nature. He compensated for the lack of his own mother's love by encouraging hugs from Louise. There were people who thought that Bob's affection for Louise was slightly obsessive, but Joan dismissed their concerns. The young mother, who was used to Singapore-paid help from locals, appreciated the way the boy watched out for her daughter. She had no reason to criticise Bob. Joan was therefore surprised when, some years later, a pre-adolescent Louise began to reject Bob's attentions. However much Joan tried to encourage Louise to include Bob in her plans, Louise started to refuse.

"He's creepy, Mummy, and he stands too close to me when I am painting. I don't like him any more." Joan expressed her disappointment to Peter.

"I have to say, Joan, I think Louise is right. She is at a stage when she needs to mix with girls of her own age. I've often thought Bob's interest in Louise was a bit odd. He's a young man now, and should be building a life of his own."

Joan very reluctantly agreed to reduce her contact with Bob. As a young child, Louise had loved Bob. He played with her toys and helped her to hold her crayons. It was Bob who helped Louise have confidence in herself and set aside her fear of men. By the time she was ten, however, she flinched when he tried to hold her hand. She pushed him away to a distance. Bob accepted his dismissal, but always harboured a desire to recapture her affection. Even when Louise left for Sussex University, he sent her cards at Christmas and birthdays, and once paid her a visit. Having met Charlie, however, he knew his ambition was impossible. He accepted his rejection, but began to compensate through fantasy, combined with self-imposed isolation. He kept a scrapbook of childhood photos of Louise, which he looked at every evening. His one advantage, he told himself in his deluded loneliness, was that he knew Louise's secret. Joan was not Louise's real mother, and Louise was not to be told.

Bob never married. When he left school, he qualified as an accountant and worked for a small finance company. He was regarded as a typical bachelor. He kept to a strict routine. He played cards with male companions every Tuesday evening, was occasionally invited to lunch with Joan and Peter, but otherwise lived a solitary life.

Joan never really understood Louise's assertion that Bob was 'creepy'. Bob had always seemed normal to her, and she enjoyed his company. When Peter died, and Joan moved to Fairlight, Joan was pleased that Bob moved to Hastings a few months later. He bought a van and spent his days visiting boot fairs and charity shops, hunting for bargains. None of his neighbours or acquaintances had been invited into his house, but they suspected he had become something of a hoarder. Joan would invite Bob for Sunday lunches, and tell him all about Louise's successes at work. She shared her disappointment with Bob, when Louise and Charlie divorced and later showed Bob photos of Louise's new studio. He would often borrow photos of Louise and offer to frame them for Joan. She was unaware that he also took copies for his expanding collection of scrapbooks.

When Joan fell ill, Bob began to feel more assertive towards her. He clung to the idea that he alone shared the secret of Louise's adoption. After years of rejection by Louise, he suddenly felt powerful. Joan's illness had made her vulnerable. He began to regard her as a broken bird in his garden, against whom he was allowed to peck. He combined his historical positive relationship with vindictive threatening, and Joan was too weak to resist. He told Joan that she owed him for keeping silent all his life about Louise's adoption.

TWENTY-THREE

Meeting Karen

Simon had returned to his house in Battle for a couple of days. He told Louise he had some business to sort out, which, in one sense, he did. He picked up the telephone and keyed in Karen's number. He had decided to use his landline to appear more credible. A female voice answered the phone.

"Hello."

"Could I speak to Mr Michael Wentworth, please?"

"Who's speaking?"

"My name is Simon Ellis."

"Just a moment please."

Simon heard Karen call her husband. "Michael, there's a guy called Simon Ellis on the phone. It might be about our glazing quote. Do you want me to deal with it?"

"No, I'd better come. It might be technical." Simon imagined Karen rolling her eyes at Michael, as she passed him the phone.

"Hello, this is Michael Wentworth."

"Oh, hi, Michael. We have met, but you may not remember me. I am Simon, a friend of Karen's cousin, Louise."

"Oh yes, she mentioned you. Is she alright?"

"She's fine, but I need your help to solve a mystery."

"Of course. What can I do for you?"

Simon took a deep breath, "Michael, do you remember at Joan's funeral you spoke to a man outside the tearoom while you were having a cigarette?"

"Vaguely," lied Michael. He remembered very well.

"That man was me."

Michael suddenly felt his heart beating in his head.

"And now, by pure coincidence, I have met Louise, and we are sort of becoming an item, and I'm a bit confused about something. You told me she is adopted. Is that true?"

"I'm not sure what to say," Michael spoke quietly. There was no time to invent a deception. "Yes, she is adopted."

"You know she doesn't know?"

"I know she doesn't know."

"So how do you know?"

"Because Karen stayed a lot with Joan and Peter shortly before and after they brought Louise home from Kent."

"Kent, not Singapore?"

"Yes, Kent."

"Why wasn't she told?"

"As far as I can remember, the welfare people said not to tell her. I'm really sorry I told you."

"Yes, I'm sorry too."

"Are you going to tell her?"

"I don't know what I'm going to do. She has dreadful nightmares about her past. I feel I am deceiving her by keeping the secret. Can I come and talk to you in Hertfordshire? It might help me decide what's best."

"Yes of course, but first I will have to tell Karen that I let out the secret. She won't be pleased."

"I'm sorry," said Simon.

"Don't be sorry, you are right. We need to talk."

Simon had a good relationship with both his sons, but more especially with his older boy, Joe. Joe was now thirty-two, and as much a friend to his father, as his offspring. They were enjoying those magical interim years when neither father or son requires a carer.

After Simon had finished the phone call with Michael, he phoned Joe.

"Hello, mate. Everything okay?" Their communication was always to the point. "Look I need to run something by you about Louise."

Joe hadn't yet met Louise, but he had heard a lot about her.

"Just marry her Dad, I don't mind. You haven't got her pregnant, have you?"

Simon rolled his eyes, "She's sixty-one years old, and I've only known her for five minutes. But, seriously, I do have a problem, and I'd like a chat."

"Sounds like this needs a couple of rounds of real ale. You can pay. I'll be at The Bull at eight this evening, after Sophie's gone to bed."

That evening the two men were sitting together in their local on Battle High Street. No one who saw them would have doubted that they were father and son. Both were tall and lean with square jaws. The younger had more hair. The older had more life experience.

Simon looked at his son and told the story of the funeral, the optician's letter, the nightmares, the phone call to Michael.

"Christ almighty, you've really got yourself into one this time. Are you sure you want to take this on? It could turn very nasty. You could walk away and just not deal with it."

Simon shook his head. "I… I really like her, Joe."

"Then it's about time I met her don't you think?"

"Okay, soon, but I don't know whether to tell her or not."

"Look, Dad you're damned if you do, and damned if you don't. If she finds out you knew and didn't tell her, that's you dumped!! It might even help you both, if she found out the truth. Less sleep walking! How have you left it with Michael?"

"I've arranged to go and see Michael and Karen without Lou knowing. I was hoping you might come with me."

Joe looked at his father for a long time. "This will cost you a lot of pints."

Simon felt very guilty about deceiving Louise. She had settled down after their last visit to Joan's bungalow, and he felt all the responsibility of the trust, which she had placed in him. He had also promised he would return to the bungalow with Louise, but neither of them had, as yet, decided when to go. Simon secretly hoped he might persuade Joe to come with them to the bungalow as well. It was a big ask, but Joe did owe him for all those years of emergency unpaid child-minding of Sophie. Simon wouldn't say that to Joe though.

In the meantime, he told Louise that Joe was coming with him on a business trip to visit a client in Hertfordshire. He said the arrangement had been made before he met Louise.

"That's a shame, I could have cadged a lift and visited my cousin, Karen."

Louise saw Simon's change of expression, "Oh sorry, Simon. You want some time alone with Joe. I was being thoughtless."

Simon invented an explanation, "Normally, I would take you along, but I have promised Joe, and I don't want him to feel you are coming between us."

"Does he think that?"

"Not at all, but I want to keep it that way."

Simon collected Joe at 8 am. Sophie, in school uniform, was standing at the door with her mother ready to wave at her grandad. Simon got out of the car and gave her a hug. "You look very smart, Sophie. Is Daddy ready?"

"He's just finishing a coffee," said Caroline. "Good luck today, Simon."

When Joe had insisted on telling Caroline the reason for their journey, Simon had at first protested.

"No more secrets, Dad, or this will get totally out of hand."

As they sped up the road, Sophie jumped up and down and waved.

"She is so lovely," smiled Simon.

"You wouldn't say that at 6 am when she jumps on the bed."

"Probably not, but I could pass her over to Louise."

It was the first time that Simon had been explicit to his son about sharing a bed with Louise, though he and Caroline had assumed they did.

"At least they can't have children of their own and disinherit you," Caroline had remarked.

The journey took over three hours. Simon drove on the understanding that Joe would take the wheel on the return trip. Joe liked to drive his Dad's Mercedes, when he got the chance. They crawled up the A21 past the roadworks at Pembury and finally emerged from the Dartford tunnel at about 10 am.

"Do you want to stop for breakfast?" asked Simon.

"Not unless you do. Let's just get there."

After a brief comfort break south of the M11, they embarked on the final leg of the journey, and soon turned off towards Sawbridgeworth. Joe had the map, in case the Sat Nav got them lost. Father and son had conversed very little during the drive, but Simon now parked in a side road and spoke, "I'm just going to ring Louise."

She answered quickly, "Hi Simon, is everything alright?"

"Fine. I just wanted you to know we have arrived at the client's. I'm running a bit late, so we need to go in."

"Okay, I won't hold you up then." Louise kept the conversation short, because she knew that Joe was in the car.

"Have you decided what you are going to say, Dad?"

"I think so, but I will have to let them take the lead."

The house in Sawbridgeworth was a large semi-detached in one of many tree-lined residential roads. It was rather a quaint place which looked like it had evolved slightly haphazardly over several decades. Simon was surprised how much he liked it. He parked his car on the newly-paved brick block drive as instructed. "This house must be worth a bit," said Joe, "We are in prime commuter land."

Michael opened the front door, and Simon and Joe climbed out of the Mercedes. Simon shook Michael's hand, "This is my older son, Joe."

Karen had watched discreetly through the window, as the two tall men approached the house. She couldn't help but be impressed by the car.

They were both offered a seat in the living room. Joe and Simon noticed a slight smell of stale cigarettes.

"Can I get you a coffee?" asked Karen, "Or tea?"

"It's a long journey for you, do you need the bathroom?" added Michael. Simon gratefully stood up, and was followed by Joe. It took ten minutes for the four of them to be seated once more with coffee cups in hand. Simon estimated that the couple were in their late seventies. They looked nervous.

"What do you need to know?" asked Michael.

"Can you tell me about the circumstances of Louise's birth?" Simon chose his words carefully.

Karen began to speak, "We know nothing about Louise's birth. Joan and Peter brought Louise back to Sawbridgeworth from Kent when she was three. I believe they collected her from a children's home in Chatham."

"She wasn't born in Singapore then?"

"No."

"How on earth was the adoption kept secret? Didn't the family and neighbours notice when Louise suddenly appeared in the house?"

"Joan and Peter had only been back in the UK a few weeks, and they had very recently purchased a house. They pretended that Louise was born in Singapore and had travelled back with them. Even Louise's grandparents believed the story."

"So why were you told?"

"Peter was a talented linguist, and he transferred to the Diplomatic Service after the war. The family always believed that Joan had married rather well. They had servants in Singapore, and returning to the UK was a bit of a shock to Joan. I was eighteen and living just around the corner from their house. Joan employed me as an unofficial mother's help. It was far better than being a shorthand typist. I was at their house the day after they brought Louise back."

"Were you the only one who knew?"

"At that time, yes, I think so. I was sworn to secrecy."

"Why was it so important to keep it a secret?"

Karen thought before responding, "This was the 1950s. There was still some shame in adoption, as most adopted babies were illegitimate. People tended not to discuss it, and I don't think Peter and Joan wanted anyone to know they couldn't have children. Peter was a bit of a snob, but he adored Louise. I also believe that the welfare people advised Joan not to tell Louise. Someone mentioned police involvement. I don't know why. We never discussed it after that. I only told Michael years later, after Peter died and Joan had moved away. I wish I hadn't now."

"Michael couldn't have known I would become friends with Louise."

"You're not going to tell her, are you? Why drag up the past?"

Simon began to feel angry.

"Do you realise that Louise has an eye test every year, because Joan had glaucoma? I hope no one in your family ever needs a transplant or the doctors might cut her up under false pretences!"

Karen and Michael exchanged glances, and Joe gave his father a kick.

Simon became calmer, "I'm sorry, but this has put me in a very difficult position. I have become very fond of Louise, and I don't want to deceive her. She has recurring nightmares about her early childhood and she has a phobia about the dark. There might be a connection with her adoption. I don't know what I'm going to do."

Just after midday, they said a courteous farewell, and Joe took the wheel of the car. He stopped at the first service station, sat his father down, and brought them both a sandwich.

"Are you alright, Dad?"

"No, I am very angry."

"It's not really Karen's fault. She was asked by Joan to keep the secret. I thought you were going to lose it big time."

"I came close. What would you do, Joe?"

Joe thought for what seemed like several minutes. "I would tell her. She has a right to know."

"I'm pleased you said that, Joe, because that is what I have definitely decided to do."

TWENTY-FOUR

Confession

Simon arrived back in Battle late that afternoon. He ate supper at Joe and Caroline's, and returned to his house. He phoned Louise.

"Are you back in Battle? Did it go well?" she asked.

"So, so. I was pleased to have Joe with me. Lou, I am very tired, so won't make it to yours this evening. I will come round first thing tomorrow morning. There's something I need to tell you."

Louise went cold. "Should I be worried?"

"Please don't worry, Lou, I will explain when I see you."

Louise worried all night.

Simon turned up at 8.30 am. Louise was already dressed and making coffee. She watched him let himself in carrying an enormous bunch of flowers.

"These are for you."

"They are beautiful, Simon. Are they connected to what you have to tell me?"

"In a way. I have deceived you, but I had a good reason."

"You're not still married?"

"No, stupid. God forbid. Look, Louise, just shut up, will you, and hear me out? This is not going to be easy, and you are going to get a shock."

The flowers lay discarded on the side of the sink. Louise sat down and was silent. Simon paced the room.

"You remember I told you that, after your mum's funeral, Michael came over and spoke to me?"

"Yes."

"Well, he didn't know that you and I would meet, so you can't really blame him, but I am a bit cross."

"Simon, you are not making sense."

"Bear with me, Lou. On the day of Joan's funeral, Michael let slip something about you. It's something you don't seem to know, something massively important."

Simon took a very deep breath, "So yesterday I lied to you. I wasn't really working. Joe and I went to visit Michael and Karen."

"How were they?" Louise asked without really thinking.

"They were fine. Will you just let me get to the point? Karen told me that you didn't go and live with Joan and Peter until you were three."

Simon paused again, "You are adopted."

Louise burst out crying. The tears poured down her cheeks, and she couldn't stop.

"Please don't cry, darling. I know this must be such a shock for you."

"I am crying with relief, Simon. I thought you were going to say we were splitting up." Louise laughed through her tears, and Simon tore off a piece of kitchen roll and handed it to her.

"I'm pleased you've got your priorities right. Louise, did you actually take in what I just told you?"

"I'm adopted. You're not leaving me, are you?"

"For God's sake, Louise, I am not ever leaving you, unless you chuck me out. You have changed my life. I love you."

She stared at him, "I love you too. I'm sorry, I can't seem to stop crying."

Louise walked over to the flowers and arranged them in a tall vase.

"These are beautiful. I should get adopted more often."

"Please don't. There is only so much kitchen roll in the world. Are you cross with me for deceiving you?"

"Cross?" I think it's wonderful that you would go all the way to Sawbridgeworth, just to find out for me. And Joe, he came with you. That was so kind."

"Any excuse to drive my car!"

The reality of what Simon had told Louise began to sink in.

"You are sure I am adopted, Simon? How did you find out?"

"Yes, I am absolutely sure."

And Simon told Louise the story of his conversation with Michael outside the café in Fairlight, and how it was a long time before he realised that Louise didn't know.

"If it hadn't been for the eye test letter, I might still believe you knew."

"Three, I was three before I was adopted? I have so much to think about."

Louise couldn't settle. She paced the floor of her studio and kept looking out of the window. She asked Simon the same questions over and over again.

"I can't make any sense of what you have told me, and yet it does make sense. Why on earth didn't they tell me?"

"I've told you that already, Louise. Asking the same question repeatedly will not provide more answers. Do you really want to know more?"

"I really want to know more."

Karen said that the police had been involved in your removal to the children's home. Are you sure you want to know? The truth might be uncomfortable."

"I have to know, Simon, as much as I can find out. Apart from anything else, it might stop these bloody nightmares."

"Well, as long as you are sure. We can start searching for clues. What else was in that folder with your school report?"

"I never looked. You seduced me, and I forgot all about it."

Simon grinned. "I haven't forgotten I seduced you."

"That's not what I meant. You know it isn't."

Simon kissed her on the mouth very deliberately. "I'm just remembering."

Louise relaxed and took the folder out of the drawer.

She skimmed through the contents.

There were three school reports, a copy of a shortened birth certificate, a black-and-white photograph, and a receipt for a £50 donation to Hellingham House in Chatham in Kent. Simon looked at the receipt, and Louise looked at the photograph. She recognised it from when Joan had showed it to her in Sawbridgeworth all those years ago. Joan's writing was now on the back. It said, '*Our precious Louise, August 1958*'.

Simon searched the internet for Hellingham House.

Wikipedia: 'Hellingham House, former children's home, which closed in the early 1980s due to increased demand for fostering. Now houses council offices and social services'

There was a photograph.

He called Louise over to look, "Is this familiar?"

"Not at all, but this is."

Louise showed Simon the black-and-white photo of a child with a suitcase. He examined it closely. It had a paperclip indent on the top right hand corner, identical to a rusty mark on the receipt from Hellingham House.

"I think this photo was once attached to this receipt."

Louise said, "The little girl in the photo is me, and I gave that suitcase to the charity shop in Fairlight the day after Mum's funeral. It was in the loft at Fairlight."

"Bloody Hell! We need it back. It might contain something useful, and it is one of the few links to your past."

Louise and Simon stared at each other.

"Do you want to go to Fairlight and try to rescue the case? We don't have to visit the bungalow as well, if that's too much for you."

"Yes, I mean maybe. Perhaps we should phone first. It was the Cancer Research shop."

Simon found the number on the internet.

"Oh yes, hello, my name is Simon Ellis. My wife, Louise, donated a small old suitcase to you a few weeks ago. We just wondered if it had sold. It has great sentimental value, and my wife has decided she would like it back. What does it look like? It's a 1950s design, brown leather, (Louise nodded), expensive looking, about the width of a briefcase, but obviously deeper."

Simon went silent and then gave the shop his mobile number. "They will ring me back. Sorry about the wife bit. I wanted to sound as credible as possible. Lou, I think we should make a plan. You need to find all the papers that your mum left. We must examine every single one for clues. Let's take a folder to the pub."

Louise gave Simon a curious look. "I do believe you are enjoying this."

"Of course not, I'm doing it for you." She looked doubtful.

"Well maybe a little. It is interesting."

"What if we discover my real parents were serial killers?"

"I will hide the kitchen knives."

Louise and Simon found Joan's folders and put them in a bag. They locked up and walked to The Ostrich for lunch.

"I need wine," announced Louise.

"I need to share your wine," Simon agreed, and they ordered a bottle of house red. Simon looked at the large bag of folders, and then the bottle. "We might need more wine."

They tucked themselves into a corner of the pub and opened a folder each. "I think we should each look at every piece of paper in case one of us misses something," instructed Simon. The arrival of lunch was an unwanted intrusion into their investigation, but they set aside their papers and ate. They had chosen extravagantly, as a mark of the importance of the occasion. Their shared platter engaged them in mutual activity, and they were diverted from the paperwork. Simon changed the subject.

"What are you doing for Christmas?"

"I have no idea."

"You are invited to Joe and Caroline's… with me of course. Oliver will come over in the evening. We can stay at my place afterwards and watch the 'no fox' hunt on Boxing Day."

Louise felt petrified at the thought of having to fit into someone else's traditional family Christmas, "That would be lovely."

Simon and Louise's motivation was dulled with the alcohol and food, but each picked up one last piece of paper. Simon examined a bank statement from Joan's final 2016 account. "Who is R. Gresham?"

"That's Bob. He's a family friend."

"Why would your mum pay him £25,000 three weeks before she died?"

"I have absolutely no idea."

Louise and Simon strolled back to the studio hand in hand. They were totally engrossed in the closeness of their relationship, and yet thrown into turmoil by the discoveries of the past few days. They laid on the bed together and fell into an immediate, deep sleep, until Louise's unconscious terrors woke Simon with her screaming.

"It's okay sweetheart, I'm here."

"Nana?"

"No, this is Simon. Let me hold you, Louise. I am here for you always."

The couple drew their bodies together and drifted back to sleep.

They were woken by the phone. Simon jumped out of bed and grabbed the handset.

"Thank you very much."

He looked at Louise, "Good news and bad. They have sold the case, but they know who bought it."

"Who bought it?" yawned Louise.

"The local primary school for a play about World War Two evacuees."

"Did you get the name of the school?"

"Chapel Lane Primary, in Guestling."

"I'll ring them."

Simon looked up the number.

Louise spoke to a voice in the school office. She explained that she had donated the case to the charity shop without realising its significance in their family history. She offered the school a donation to funds, if they would return the case. The voice said she would ring Louise back.

"All this waiting is so frustrating," Louise said to Simon.

"You'd better get used to it, Lou. I suspect there is a lot more to come."

The school rang back quickly. Louise answered, while Simon watched her changing expressions. She seemed to be listening for ages.

"What time tomorrow would be convenient?"

She scribbled down a name and ended the call.

Simon waited for Louise to speak.

"They have the case. We can collect it tomorrow at 10 am. But there's more, Simon. One of the children found an old photo in a side pocket of the case. The teacher kept it and was going to use it as inspiration for creative writing. The photo is of a lady standing outside a house. There is a word written on the back. She said it's a bit faded but still legible. It says 'Nana'."

Once again, Simon and Louise stared at each other. Louise exhaled loudly, and Simon hugged her for a very long time.

Louise slept badly that night. She was worried she might be invaded by dreams.

"I can't dream if I stay awake all night."

"Try and relax. I am here with you." Simon's reassurance was useless. Louise got up and spent the rest of the night painting. Eventually, Simon went back to sleep. He would need to be strong for both of them.

TWENTY-FIVE

From Guestling to Battle

B y ten past nine, they were in the car ready to leave.

"Louise, have you got your cheque book and the cash?"

She double-checked in her handbag.

"Yes."

They headed towards Guestling. The plan was to visit the school and then make a brief visit to the bungalow in Fairlight.

They arrived at the school at a quarter to ten. Simon parked outside on the road, and they waited in the car until a few minutes before ten. They found the main entrance and rang the bell. The intercom spoke.

"Can I help you?"

"It's Mrs Watson about the photo… and of course the suitcase."

They were buzzed in. A lady behind the reception desk asked them to sit and wait. They lowered themselves into the lightly upholstered chairs and looked at the childish art on the walls. Louise tried to distract herself.

"These are good. I like that one with the colourwash over the crayon."

A lady appeared with the suitcase, and Simon took Louise's hand.

"Mrs Watson, I believe this belongs to you."

"Thank you so much. Have you got the photograph?"

The secretary produced a small white envelope, which she handed to Louise.

"It's lucky the class teacher decided to keep it."

Louise's hand trembled, as she opened the envelope. It revealed a tall, smartly dressed, lady in 1950s clothing. She was standing outside an elegant Victorian house. On the back was written the word 'Nana'.

"Do you know this lady?" asked the secretary, "She looks a lot like you."

Louise's eyes filled with tears.

"I'm sorry, I'm a bit emotional. I'm adopted you see. I think this lady may be a birth relative."

Simon took over.

"Can you please thank the teacher for us. This is a very big moment for Louise." He took forty pounds from his own wallet.

"We want to make a donation to your school."

"You really don't have to."

"We want to."

"Perhaps, when your wife feels better, she could give us a ring and tell us a bit more. I'm sure the children would love to know the whole story."

"We'll do that," said Simon. He picked up the case and ushered Louise back to the car. She gripped the photo.

"I keep thinking that the lady in my dreams may have touched this photo."

"It's mind blowing, Louise. I'm sorry people keep assuming we are married. We must behave like an old married couple."

"Less of the old," Louise grinned. "Thank you, Simon for being so understanding. I really couldn't do this without your support. Charlie would have grown very cross with me by now."

"I'm here for you Louise… but you do now owe me forty pounds. Can you cope with Fairlight?"

"Why not?"

Simon swung the car around and turned into the narrow lane which led to the Fairlight Road.

He drove gently through the country roads until he reached the steep hill which approached Fairlight village. The sky was cloudless, and they could see the fields and coastline stretching to Dungeness in the distance.

"That is some view, a bit clearer than on the day of your mother's funeral."

"Let's hope it's a good omen."

Simon parked outside the bungalow.

"I want you to stay locked in the car. I'm going to walk round the bungalow and check it out before we go in."

"What if someone is there?"

"Then I will run like hell."

Simon approached the bungalow with a confident manner, while Louise was watching. Once out of her sight he slowed down and took his mobile phone out of his pocket as an extra precaution. His steps were tentative, and he looked around constantly. The wooden insert with which he had secured the patio door from the inside was still in place. All the windows were closed, and he could see no sign of intrusion. He walked back to the car.

"It looks fine, Lou, but I'm going inside to check every room before you come in."

"You don't need to baby me, Simon."

"Yes, I do. It makes me feel manly."

Louise was more than happy to comply. Simon unlocked the front door and glanced into the lounge. The front of the desk was closed. He looked in Louise's bedroom. There was no photo on the bed. He went back to the living area and opened the desk. The photo was still in the desk. After a brief check of the other rooms, Simon returned to Louise.

"Everything seems fine. You wanna come in?"

Louise was still holding the photograph. She returned it to the envelope, slipped it in her handbag, and got out of the car.

"Just for five minutes."

They walked around the bungalow and felt a sense of relief.

"Perhaps it was just kids, after all."

Once they had double-checked every lock, they returned to Robertsbridge.

Simon made some coffee, while Louise re-examined the photo.

"I've got some software at my house which might be able to pick out a few more details on that photo. It would do us both good, I think, to have a change of scene for a couple of days. You can bring the case and all the paperwork with you. I know you won't be able to stop thinking about it, and it's about time you stayed with me."

"I'll need some time to pack."

"And I'll need some time on my own to warm up the house. I'll come back for you, shall I? Or you could drive over later, then you will have your own car with you."

You are so thoughtful, Simon, why didn't I find you earlier?"

"Sadly, I haven't always been this thoughtful. Ring me before you leave, and I will put the kettle on."

As Louise watched Simon's car disappear, she began to feel nervous. Despite their original plans, Louise had not yet visited Simon's house. The events of the past days had overtaken them. She looked at the calendar on her phone. It was only three weeks since they met at the garden centre. It seemed much longer. He was right to suggest she took her own car. She needed to feel safe. She might not like staying at his house. She might meet his sons, his neighbours, his ex-wife even. She wondered if she had time for a shower. She would make time.

It took Louise two hours to shower, dry her hair, pack a case, and put the papers into a holdall. The photograph was in her handbag. She carried her belongings downstairs in two journeys and phoned Simon from her car.

"I'm just nipping to the cash machine and then I'll be with you."

"I don't charge rent."

Simon was watching nervously from an upstairs window, when Louise arrived. As instructed, she parked her car next to his in the drive. Simon was pleased that Louise had taken her time. He had contacted his cleaner and offered her twice her normal rate, if she could come round immediately. In the space of two hours Mrs Simms had changed the bed, cleaned the bathrooms and wiped over the kitchen, while Simon had escaped into Battle. He purchased a few provisions as well as two night lights, which he put on the dressing table in his bedroom.

He opened the front door and kissed Louise.

"Welcome to Chez Simon. Sorry, that sounds rather clichéd."

Louise looked at the front garden.

"This is beautiful."

His nerves eased a little, "Let me take your case upstairs. I'll show you the bedroom. You look lovely by the way."

He led the way. "I hope this is alright. I don't have a dressing table, but you can use this chest of drawers for your make-up and hair, and I've cleared some space in the wardrobe or would you rather put your things in the spare room… and I bought two night lights."

Louise laughed out loud.

"Simon, it's lovely. I love the house and I'm very adaptable, and thank you for making so much effort. Now where's that kettle?"

"Sorry, I just wanted it to be right. This is a man-house. You might find it a bit clinical."

Suddenly, Louise felt the need to take charge. She sighed loudly.

"Go downstairs, make me a cup of tea, and I will join you in a few minutes. I just want to hang up a couple of tops."

He did as he was told.

After tea, Simon showed Louise round the house and garden and confessed about his panic phone call to the cleaner. They sat back down, and he asked, "Pub or takeaway?"

"Which would you prefer?"

"Well I do want to talk to you. I have a proposition, so how about a takeaway? You choose."

Simon handed Louise a massive pile of takeaway delivery leaflets.

"These are essential for a man who lives alone."

By the time the food delivery arrived, Simon and Louise were sitting at the kitchen table sharing a bottle of wine.

"Have you thought what you are going to do about finding out more about your biological family?"

"I have moments when I think I will do nothing. My real mum is probably dead by now and I have the photo as a link to the past."

Simon looked momentarily disappointed.

"The problem is," Louise continued "I can't seem to let it go. I think about it all the time. I guess I will have to try and find out more."

By this time, they were helping themselves to portions of fried rice, vegetables and chilli beef from plastic containers. Simon refilled Louise's glass.

"Do you want to go and see Karen?"

"I know it's not really her fault, but I feel very cross with Karen. All those years she was holding a secret which belonged to me. I don't think I can face her yet."

"I have to confess that I felt cross with Karen on your behalf when I met her with Joe. Karen said you were collected from a children's home in Kent, and the receipt in your mum's papers was for a donation to Hellingham House in Chatham, Kent. There must be a connection. If we could find a bit more information we could go there. Maybe stay in a hotel and have a few days away together? I hear that Chatham dockyard is well worth a visit."

Louise considered his proposal.

"I might get very emotional, Simon. Are you sure you can put up with me?"

"You can't do this on your own, Lou, and you do have good reason to be emotional. I think I'd be far more worried if you didn't show emotion."

Simon hesitated, "I'm not sure if you'll like me admitting this, but I'm rather looking forward to the research. It's my sort of project."

"I actually feel a lot better knowing I'm not being a nuisance. The only thing is, I don't want to be put under pressure. You will have to let me dictate the pace."

Simon grinned and stroked Louise's hand.

"You are getting to know me a bit too well. I do get carried away sometimes. You must tell me, if I am moving too quickly… with anything. I promise I will listen and slow down."

They filled the bin with left overs and plastic containers and loaded the dishwasher. Louise suddenly became very tired. She sat on the sofa and felt her eyes closing.

"You've had an exhausting day, Lou. Why don't you go to bed? I'll come up in a minute and say goodnight."

By the time Simon went upstairs to see Louise, she was fast asleep. He stood and watched her sleeping body in the dim glow of his newly-purchased nightlight.

"You have a woman in your bed, Simon," he said to himself with satisfaction.

He crept downstairs, turned on his computer and did another search for Hellingham House.

Hellingham House, Chatham, Kent,
Address: 27, Moor Lane, Chatham, ME4
Tel. 01634 879622
Opening hours 9.30–4 pm Mon to Thurs

He wondered where Louise had left the photograph from the suitcase. He would ask her in the morning. The phone rang. It was Joe.

"Shush, I have a sleeping visitor. You will wake her up."

"Sorry, Dad, I didn't realise her bedtime was so early."

"It's not everyday you find a photo of a long-lost relative. It's very tiring."

And Simon explained to Joe about the suitcase and the photograph.

"Am I boring you?"

"No, Dad, seriously, you're not. It's fascinating, but I do have something to tell you. Oliver has heard that Louise is staying, and he wants to visit."

"That's all I need. Is he going to be difficult?"

"Possibly, and he'll just turn up. I thought I should warn you."

"Thanks Joe, I'll fill Louise in tomorrow."

Simon climbed the stairs and found his pyjamas neatly folded on the pillow next to Louise's head. He changed in the bathroom, so as not to wake her. When he returned, she was enveloped in the duvet, and he could not untangle her.

"Duvet wars, is it?" whispered Simon. He grabbed a blanket from the spare room, and covered himself on the bed beside her.

TWENTY-SIX

Meeting Oliver

The doorbell rang at 8.30 am the following morning. Simon had finally gained possession of his share of the duvet, and they were relaxing in bed with a coffee and their laptops. Louise was reading Simon's link about Hellingham House, and Simon was researching hotels in Chatham.

"Bloody Hell, who's that?" groaned Simon, when he heard the bell. "If it's blokes offering to tarmac my drive on the cheap, I might thump them."

He pulled on some joggers and went downstairs.

He opened the door to his younger son, Oliver.

"Hi, Dad, I just wondered how you are?"

Simon poured Oliver a coffee and sat him in the lounge.

"I'll be back in a minute."

He hurried upstairs.

"Lou, I'm really sorry, but my younger son, Oliver, is here. He lives with his mother. I should have told you more about him and about my divorce, but it never seemed the right time."

Louise shot out of bed and grabbed some clothes.

"You go down, I'll be with you in a minute… unless you want me to escape through the back window."

"Don't be daft. We have to face this. I would just have preferred a bit of planning time."

Louise brushed her hair and added a flash of lipstick. She calmly walked downstairs into the lounge. She offered Oliver her hand.

"Hello, Oliver. It's good to meet you."

Oliver was in his mid-twenties and very good looking, despite the sceptical expression on his face.

"So you are the woman who is about to become my stepmother."

Simon felt his anger rising. He knew his younger son was being intentionally provocative. He stood up and was close to exploding. Louise sensed Simon's increasing negative emotions. She thought quickly.

"Well your father hasn't actually asked me to marry him yet, but it is a possibility."

Simon sat down again in surprise.

"So maybe you'd better tell me all about yourself, Oliver. I'm not going to accept anyone as a stepson."

Simon was astounded. He had never seen Louise this confident.

"I was only joking," mumbled Oliver.

"Well I wasn't," continued Louise, "Tell me about yourself. You're obviously an early riser. Simon and I were still in bed."

Oliver stuttered. "I was on my way to Hastings, and I thought I'd drop in."

"It's really lovely to meet you. Can I get you some breakfast? We've got some bacon haven't we, Simon?"

Oliver was so surprised by Louise that he accepted the offer of breakfast. Simon opened the bacon. A few minutes later they were all sitting in the kitchen eating bacon sandwiches. Louise kept talking.

"So when are we going to see you again? I'm only staying for a few days, so how about tomorrow? You could come for dinner."

"I think I'm busy tomorrow. Can I text you, Dad?"

"Of course, son."

And Oliver was gone.

Simon sat down on the hall floor and gazed at Louise.

"That was one of the most impressive performances I've ever seen. How on earth did you do it? I thought you would fall apart. Oliver can be very provocative."

"My dear Simon, I have spent over thirty years dealing with stroppy teenagers in a classroom. You just have to stand up to them and call their bluff. Oliver may be older than the kids I taught, but he was no different. He wanted me to crumble. Do you think I've upset him?"

"I should think he's in shock. His mother would never stand up to him like that, but you did it so... charmingly."

"Simon, perhaps it's time you told me a bit more about your first marriage?"

"I agree, but you must promise not to be too hard on me."

Simon made another two mugs of coffee and settled in the living room with Louise. He told her how he had met Julie in the summer of 1980, a few years after he graduated. He was working for a large computer company as a systems analyst. Julie was a junior secretary, and Simon was impressed with her warm, friendly manner and stunning good looks. They married in 1981. Julie worked part-time until their sons, Joe and then Oliver, were born a few years later. She then gave up work to be a full-time mum. Simon believed he was an attentive husband and caring father. He worked hard to provide his family with everything that Julie wanted. With the emergence of the worldwide web, and the need for more skilled computer personnel, he was rapidly promoted. In the late 1990s Simon left his job and set up his own website design company. He was very knowledgeable and a good manager of his new and growing team. His timing was perfect. Within five years Simon was turning over several million pounds and employing over fifty junior website designers. During these years, he worked long hours and became increasingly focussed on developing his business. His wife, Julie, with no job of her own and no desire to pursue a career, began to feel neglected. The boys grew up, both sets of grandparents had died, and her perceived role in the family diminished. She was, however, still an attractive woman.

In 2010 Simon came home early from work and discovered his wife in bed with another man. Julie begged for his forgiveness and promised the affair was over, but, however hard Simon tried, he could not forget her transgression. In 2012 he asked for a divorce. He sold the business, gave Julie an income and the family home in Ninfield, and bought himself a substantial pension. He purchased the house in Battle, close to his older son, Joe and his family. Oliver stayed in Ninfield with his mother. Since the divorce, Julie had made every attempt to turn her younger son against his father, but despite occasional hostility, Simon had managed to maintain a relationship with Oliver.

However, even with Joe close by and with considerable financial security in retirement, Simon had not coped well with the adjustment to a life which had changed so suddenly. He was lonely and felt restless, now without full-time work or marriage.

"Are you sure you don't want to go back to her? After all, it's only been a few years," Louise asked fearfully.

"I could never go back, Lou. I know I seem pretty easy going, but I find it difficult to forgive people, when they really hurt me. I felt like that, on your behalf, when I met Karen and discovered what she had hidden from you."

Simon went into the kitchen to clear away. In his head he could still hear Louise's words to Oliver about marriage. "Well it is a possibility," Louise had said. Louise followed the sound of scraping plates and watched Simon bend over the dishwasher and slide the crockery into the rack. He sensed her presence, turned round and kissed her. "There is something about you I want to take issue with."

"What?"

"You are a stealer of duvets. I had to get a blanket last night."

Louise giggled, "I do tend to wrap myself up when I'm tired."

He kissed her again, and moved his hand inside her shirt. He sensed inner arousal from deep within her body.

"I think you and I need to practise duvet sharing. Shall we try now?" She kissed him very deliberately and led him by the hand towards the kitchen door. He stroked her back as he followed her upstairs and sat on the bed beside her. He gently unbuttoned her top and unclipped her bra. He stroked her breasts and moved his mouth over her each of her nipples before laying her down on the bed. She helped him to remove the remainder of their clothing, between kisses. He picked up the duvet, covered her body and climbed under the bedclothes beside Louise. Simon felt a renewed confidence as he eagerly began to explore her innermost places with his fingers and his lips.

"I love you, Louise Watson."

"I love you, Simon Ellis."

Their love making was long and hard and tender.

When they finally emerged, it was almost midday.

Louise wanted to cook an evening meal in Simon's kitchen. She walked into Battle to shop for food. Simon was banished from the trip, so he asked Louise if he could borrow the photograph of Nana to examine, while Louise was shopping. He printed two photocopies then scanned the original photograph into his computer. The photo was then placed safely back in the envelope.

He enlarged the scan. There was no sign of a road name, but he could see the number nine on the front door. It was a start. He opened a free version of his location search software. *Search for property… browse your computer… enter.* The software threw up 7000 matches. *Refine search… Kent.* 600 matches. That was a bit better. He switched on his printer and produced a list. How on earth was he to sift through so much information?

TWENTY-SEVEN

The Return of Bob

As Bob approached retirement, he began to have problems with his knees. The hospital recommended knee replacement, but Bob could not be persuaded to undergo the surgery. He made medical excuses to Joan, but she suspected that he was afraid of the after-care. When Bob first moved to Hastings, Joan had called at his house, but he had not invited her in, preferring to talk to her on the doorstep. Joan soon realised that Bob never let anyone inside his house. A knee replacement would have necessitated home visits from both a carer and a district nurse, and Bob could not have coped with the intrusion. Joan occasionally asked Bob what he would do if his knees got worse, but he always changed the subject.

When Louise finally split up with Charlie, Bob had hoped to spend more time with her, but he soon discovered that his knees would not allow him to access Louise's studio. He found the stairs very difficult to climb, and had to stop and rest several times when he attempted them. Louise was relieved, because she thought he might have become a nuisance. She always claimed a prior engagement, when Bob invited her out somewhere else for a coffee or lunch, and he eventually stopped asking. He occasionally encountered Louise at Joan's bungalow, but noticed that Louise did not stay long, if he was there.

Joan had not been surprised by her diagnosis of cancer. She

had felt increasing discomfort in her stomach over several months, and no amount of self-medication offered relief. It was only when the pain became severe, and she began to feel breathless that she visited her GP. Despite the immediate referral to hospital, it was too late for the consultant to offer any solution other than palliative care. The prognosis was estimated at about six months. Joan invited Louise for tea at the De La Warr Pavilion. She was still driving at the time, and arranged to meet Louise in the upstairs café. Joan wanted to tell Louise in a public space to avoid too many tears. She knew her daughter cried easily, but would be better controlled, if on view. She had judged the situation well. Joan delivered a well-rehearsed speech to Louise, and watched her blink back the tears.

"Can't they do anything, Mum?" asked Louise.

"It's better this way," replied Joan. "I don't want to be poked about and opened up just to give me a few more months."

Louise suspected her mother had delayed treatment on purpose. "What did Bob say?"

"I haven't told him yet. I wanted to tell you first." Louise was grateful that Joan had assigned her priority.

When Joan finally explained the situation to Bob, he seemed annoyed that Joan had told Louise first. He wanted to have a role in comforting Louise, but felt excluded. He began to regard Joan as the enemy and slowly convinced himself that it was Joan who had prevented him from getting closer to Louise. As Joan grew weaker, Bob gained a sense of self-importance. He started to enjoy the psychological power he could exert over Joan. Unable to admit to Louise that she had been right about Bob, Joan pretended that all was well. She allowed Bob to abuse her verbally and told no-one about his unkindness.

"It's a good thing that Peter is dead," Bob would frequently say. "He wouldn't want to see you looking like this. Your face has grown ugly with the cancer." Joan was too tired to argue with Bob. Fortunately, her final two weeks were spent in a hospice, and she gave instructions that only family should be allowed to visit.

After Joan died, Bob decided that now was the time to revive his relationship with Louise. Louise would inherit sufficient money to buy somewhere more accessible, and she would undoubtedly be grateful for the attention he had paid to Joan in her later years. He imagined his old age sitting in a seafront conservatory holding Louise's hand. In his solitude, the fantasy had become very real. He began to drive regularly to Robertsbridge and park somewhere hidden, where he could take secret photos of Louise, as she left her studio. He still had a key to Joan's bungalow, and made occasional visits. He was determined that at some stage he would surprise Louise by climbing the stairs at the studio. He waited a month until after Joan's funeral and then drove on a mission to Robertsbridge. He had taken several pain killers and smothered his knees in analgesic gel in order to negotiate the stairs. He reached the ground floor front door and knocked loudly several times. Eventually, Doreen from the downstairs maisonette opened the ground floor entrance door.

"Sorry to disturb you. Is Louise in?"

"I'm afraid not, dear. She's gone to stay with her young man."

"Young man?" Bob began to twitch. He knew nothing about Simon.

"Well yes. He isn't really young, I suppose, but he seems young to me," explained Doreen.

"I've got something for her. It's a surprise. Could you let me in so I can leave it in the studio for her?"

"And you are?"

"Bob, I've known Louise since she was three."

"I don't think I can give you the key, Bob, but if you leave whatever it is with me, I'll see she gets it. She said she would only be away for a few days… probably."

"Thank you, but that would spoil the surprise. I'll wait 'til she gets back." And Bob watched Doreen retire back into her lobby. She moved very slowly, and he glimpsed the rack of keys hanging in her hallway. Bob limped back to his car and drove home.

TWENTY-EIGHT

Journey to Chatham

In late November 2016, after a few days apart, Simon collected Louise from Robertsbridge, and they set off for Chatham. It was the week before the start of Advent, and they drove past a gathering congregation beginning to decorate the area surrounding the village memorial. They didn't notice Bob's car parked at a safe distance waiting for them to leave. Simon turned on the radio to hear the local traffic news. They listened in the car for a few minutes, then turned off the radio. Simon broke the silence.

"Are you alright, Lou? I've missed you."

"I've missed you too, but I did have to go home and prepare for our trip."

"Did you manage to do any painting?"

"No. My mind was too active. I've brought a few paints with me, though. I thought I might get a couple of sketches done at the dockyard."

"And your nightmares?"

"Worst they've ever been."

"I'm so sorry, sweetheart. I feel responsible. Are you sure you feel strong enough to do this?"

"You don't have to keep asking me, Simon. I am able to make my own decisions."

"Sorry."

They stopped for a late lunch just outside of Rochester, then drove to the hotel in Chatham. Simon had insisted on paying for a suite for the five days.

"When we go on our world cruise, you can pay," he told Louise.

Louise and Simon had not discussed their finances in detail, but she suspected he had money to spare. It was a modern hotel, and the room was beautiful. It had a large marble bathroom and separate lounge area. They had plenty of space. Their house sharing time together had helped them to adjust to each other's routines. They knew who would have which side of the bed and allowed each other space to unpack.

"Wow," Louise finally admitted, "This suite is amazing. I think I'll investigate my adoption more often." Simon put his arm around Louise with affection. She suddenly felt grateful he was in his sixties. Simon would take his lead from Louise and would not overwhelm her with physical demands. She remembered being immediately pounced on by Charlie every time they had entered a hotel room. She knew Simon would keep his distance for the rest of the day. He would need to rest after the drive, and Louise needed to think.

Simon lay on the bed and connected his laptop to the free wifi, while Louise made them both a coffee. She looked out of the seventh floor window and realised she could see the estuary. She moved a chair in front of the window, put a small plastic mat on the floor and set up her portable easel. After they had both finished their coffee, Simon fell asleep, and Louise lost herself in her painting.

The following morning, they had an appointment with the senior administrator at Hellingham House. They ate a substantial breakfast and left plenty of time for the short car ride. The building was well signposted as Hellingham House, KCC Social Services. Simon turned into the tree-lined gravel drive and pulled in to one side.

"I'm just giving you time to absorb this, Lou. You have an amazing visual memory, so something might register."

"I don't feel like I've been here before. Let's keep going."

Simon parked in the small tarmacked car park. They stood

beside the car and looked at the building. To the left was a large extension with offices, not really in keeping with the original architecture. Louise held up her photograph from Joan's folder and compared it with their view.

"This is definitely it. The extension wasn't there, and the windows are new, but the original porch is still here. Look how small I am in the photo in comparison to the doorway, and I was tall for my age. It's almost time. Shall we knock?"

They approached the impressive entrance and pressed the intercom.

"Louise Watson, here to see Mr Burton."

They were buzzed in. The hallway was grand with original plasterwork on the Victorian ceilings. Louise wanted to recognise something. She wanted to please Simon for his efforts, but there was no sense of the familiar.

A man arrived and held out his hand. "Mrs Watson, welcome to Hellingham House. I am Matthew Burton." He turned to Simon, "And you are?"

"Simon Ellis, a friend."

"Good. It is always important to have support on these occasions."

Matthew led the way to a comfortable reception room. "Please sit down. I do have some information for you, but first I need to ask some questions. Have you got your ID?"

Louise produced her passport. "And are you happy for Mr Ellis to be included in the disclosure?"

"Yes."

"Can I call you Louise?" Louise nodded.

"I am the senior administrator here. I have overall responsibility for personnel, health and safety and finance, but my most rewarding job is dealing with historical adoption queries. I have to warn you that the information which I disclose to applicants can sometimes be very distressing. Are you certain you want to continue?"

"I am certain."

Simon gripped Louise's hand.

"We do have a list of counselling services which you can access, if you think it would help."

Simon was growing impatient, but he held his tongue.

"How old are you Louise?"

"I'm sixty-one."

"Most of our applicants are much younger. Why did you wait so long?"

"My mother died a few weeks ago. I only discovered from a cousin recently that I was adopted. This paper and photograph were in a file at my mother's house." She stopped to think before continuing, "I get nightmares, unexplained flashbacks from my early childhood. I need to know my history."

"I can't promise to tell you a lot, but I do have a couple of pieces of the jigsaw. We found your admission and exit record in our archives. The files have recently been reorganised following an allegation of child abuse at the home during the sixties. I suspect you may have escaped just in time. I have copied the papers for you."

Inside a plastic wallet were several documents. "Can I get you a coffee or tea?" They nodded. Matthew picked up a phone and requested refreshments. He was not allowed to leave the couple alone.

Louise read the first piece of paper.

28th July 1958: Louise Makepiece admitted

Mother: Patricia Makepiece, deceased

Next of kin:(Grandmother) Catherine Makepiece, incompetent, Address: 9, Penhurst Crescent, Rochester, Kent

Responsible Adult: Ruby Makepiece (cousin), address: 24, London Road, Dartford, Kent

Transported by Constable Richards, Kent Police

Louise passed the first paper to Simon.

The next paper read.

Adoption Certificate: *19th October 1958*

It is hereby certified that Mr and Mrs P. Watson of 31, Sheering Mill Drive, Sawbridgeworth, are assigned formal adoption rights to Louise Patricia Watson DOB 22nd July 1955.

Signed A. Mills, Registrar at Hellingham House.

Louise looked at Matthew.

I was adopted in October?"

"That's the date on the certificate. I would imagine that Mr and Mrs Watson collected you some months earlier."

"What does incompetent mean?"

"It's an old-fashioned welfare word for mental-health issues, learning difficulties, alcohol problems, even prostitution. To be honest, Louise, you are extremely fortunate that we have this much information. Keeping birth information about adoptees was not encouraged in the 1950s because of the shame of illegitimacy. Your adopted father, Peter Watson, made a substantial donation to the home. It's likely that they kept him on file in case they should decide to ask for more."

Louise found a carbon copy of the receipt which had been in Joan's file. "Thank you, Dad," she said.

"So am I definitely illegitimate?"

"Nothing is certain, but there is no mention of a father, so it seems probable. My guess is that your birth mother died, and your grandmother took you in. It is only a guess though.

"I think this is my grandma." Louise produced the photo of 'Nana'. "She doesn't look like an alcoholic, does she?"

Matthew showed some unguarded emotion and grinned, "No, Louise. It is difficult to match that photo with the word 'incompetent'."

"Do you have any more questions?"

"I don't think so. Can I please take a photo of this room? I don't recognise anywhere else, but this room feels familiar."

"Of course. I would offer to show you upstairs where the children's living quarters were, but it has been completely gutted and turned into offices. I don't think a tour would help. Feel free to take photos outside. I wish you every success with your quest." Louise took a few photos of the room, and they left the building.

Simon took a few more photos of the porch. "Lou, I know this sounds mad, but I've brought the case with us. Hold the handle, go and stand in the same place, and I will take another photo of you. 'Then and now'."

And Simon directed Louise to stand holding the case in the exact spot where she stood at the age of three. He took several photos.

"Time to leave now, I think," said Simon, "How do you feel?"

"I feel like someone has given me an extra piece of my life."

They had only been at Hellingham House for about two hours, but Louise was so tired that she could barely speak. Simon was pleased that he had purchased the extra space in the hotel. On their return, Louise lay on the king-size bed and fell immediately fast asleep. Simon opened his computer on the table in the living area. While his laptop warmed up, he looked at the watery outlines on Louise's easel. He was stunned by the effect that a few lines could have on a blank sheet of paper. She had transported the dockyard onto the page. Simon could only guess how much comfort her painting brought to her in times of anguish.

He opened the plastic folder of papers and entered the last known address of Catherine Makepiece into google maps. It threw up a map of Rochester. He switched to 'streetview', and a photo of a crescent of large Victorian terraced houses appeared on screen. Most of the houses appeared to be converted to flats. He took out the list of Kent addresses, which his computer had linked to the photograph of Nana's house. The address in Rochester was there. He finally plucked up the courage to compare the photo of the house with Nana with the photo on his screen of the address from Hellingham House. It was an undoubted match. Louise's grandma, Nana, and probably Louise as well, had lived in 9, Penhurst Crescent, Rochester.

Louise woke up at three o clock in the afternoon. Simon made her a cup of tea.

"We seem to take turns at sleeping through lunch. I'm sorry, Simon, you must be hungry."

"Not at all. I have been making discoveries," and Simon showed Louise the google photograph of the house in Rochester.

She used the mouse to turn the streetview photograph around at angles and examine every detail.

They had three days left at the hotel. Louise insisted that they take some time out before seeking out the house in Rochester. She needed to regain her emotional strength, and she wanted Simon to have a break. So the following day, they visited Chatham dockyard. They explored the Rope Yard, took a trip inside the depths of a nuclear submarine, and Louise set up her easel and painted, while Simon climbed aboard a second world war navy gunboat. The day removed them from their mission and renewed their energy. That evening they ate dinner together in the hotel.

Simon found the courage to speak.

"Louise, you know I love you, don't you?"

"I do hope so, Simon, because I have so much to thank you for."

"I don't want your gratitude, Lou, just your company. And I'm not trying to rush you, but this nomadic life living in two homes is very tiring. I know it is too soon, but if... when... you feel ready, I do hope we can move in together."

She looked down momentarily and reflected on her reply, "It's true we've not been together long at all, but we have packed an awful lot into a short time. I never thought I'd say this, but I'm not getting any younger and I don't think I will cope with those steps up to the studio much longer. I'm going to have to sell it. My mum, I mean Joan, would say she told me so. It's going to take a lot of thought, but I would like it if you were included in my future plans."

"I want us to plan our future together, Lou, not 'if', but 'when'. Promise me you will include me in the next phase of your life... our life."

"I promise. I really, truly promise."

The extra security of the conversation gave them strength for the next day.

Nana haunted Louise's sleep. She painted the walls with rainbows and danced over the bed. She finally locked Louise in the darkness of the hotel wardrobe, and Louise sat upright with a very loud scream.

"Louise, wake up. The hotel staff will think I am murdering you."

"Oh, I'm so sorry, Simon. I hate it when this happens."

"Let me hold you in my arms. You might feel more secure."

Louise drifted back to sleep, with gentle dreams of Joan in the room at Hellingham House.

Simon was pleased that she was calm, but spent the next hour trying to remove his arm from under her back without waking her up.

"Be careful what you wish for, Simon," he laughed to himself. "This is the woman who steals your duvet. She is now removing all the circulation from your arm."

The following day brought rain. It bounced off the hotel car park and invaded the hotel lobby. Louise and Simon delayed their breakfast in the hope of a reprieve, but the rain was determined to fill up the day.

"Bloody Kent weather," mumbled Simon. He wrapped his lists and printed map in a carrier bag and tucked them inside his coat.

"I'll bring the car round to the front," he said to Louise, "You wait in the entrance."

The commissionaire intercepted him.

"Would you like me to bring your car around to the front entrance for you, sir?"

"Yes, please," said Simon, and he handed over his keys.

"The power of a suite," remarked Simon to Louise, "But I have no idea how much to tip him."

"Don't ask me," Louise said, "I don't think he'd have offered to drive my Astra."

Someone from reception sheltered them under a large umbrella on the short route to Simon's car.

"I could get used to this," Simon whispered to Louise, as he fumbled for some change from his pocket.

They drove the two miles to Rochester, still laughing about their elevated status.

They easily found Penhurst Crescent. It was an elegant road not far from the Church. Simon managed to park, and they walked hand in hand in the rain until they found number nine. Louise took a photo. "If I wasn't so involved, I would paint this road. It's beautiful."

The tall Victorian or possibly Edwardian house had been converted into flats. There were four doorbells on the entry phone. There was no point in ringing any of the bells.

"My grandma lived here," announced Louise to Simon, "I lost touch with her, but I believe she was special."

"I'm sure she was remarkable."

"Is this the end of our search, Simon?"

"It might be, but don't give up yet, Lou. I have a few ideas."

They hurried back to the car in the increasingly torrential Kent rain.

That evening they sat in their hotel suite and watched the weather forecast. There would be more rain the following day with sunshine predicted on the morning of their departure. The dockyard was preparing for its winter closure, but they agreed to return anyway on their last full day and to make a short final visit to Penhurst Crescent before driving home on the Friday. Simon would visit the Lifeboat Collection, and Louise wanted to look at the pictures in the gift shop to see if it was worth offering them any of hers.

"I don't make much profit," she explained to Simon, "But the sales do help with the cost of materials."

They then sat and wrote a list of questions about Louise's adoption, which they wanted to pursue.

Could they trace Ruby? What relation was she to Louise?

What happened to Catherine? Why was she described as 'incompetent'?

Could they access the deeds to the house in Penhurst Crescent?

How did Patricia die?

Would the police have any records which might help?

"I don't know how we should go about this, Lou. I do know you can employ an agency to help, but I bet it's expensive. We'll have to do some research when we get home."

On the Friday, as planned, they returned to Rochester. The sun was shining and the whole area looked even more desirable. Simon and Louise stood outside number nine Penhurst Crescent and scrutinised the house.

I'd say it's now divided into four flats. Shame one of them isn't up for sale, we could go and look round.

"You are very devious, Simon."

An elderly man walked past them.

"This crescent used to be the pride of Rochester. Look at it now. Our country's gone downhill."

"Do you live here?"

"Goodness, no. I couldn't manage all those stairs. They have no lifts you know. I have a retirement flat near the docks."

"Do you, by any chance, know anyone who lives in this road?" asked Simon.

"Sorry no. Are you looking to buy one? Investors, are you?"

"I think my grandmother owned number nine in the fifties. I'm trying to trace my family history."

"She'd have been wealthy then, your grandma. These were prestigious family homes in the fifties. Have you tried the library?"

"No."

"Rochester library has a massive reference section. My late wife and I traced the history of our last house through the records in the library. And don't forget the museum. They have loads of local history. Better get there before government cuts close it."

"The museum or the library?"

"Both."

"Are they planning to close them?"

"No, but with this government it'll probably happen."

Simon squeezed Louise's hand. "Well thank you for your help."

Simon and Louise walked away.

Louise started to laugh.

"Shush, he'll hear you. We'd better get to the library before the government close it! It was good advice though. Looks like we might need another trip to Rochester."

Louise cast a final look at the house, and they walked, hand in hand, back to the car.

Simon offered Louise his car keys. "Do you want to drive?"

He hoped she would refuse.

"I don't really want to drive your car, Simon. It's too large."

"And I don't want you to drive it. I just thought I should offer." He opened the passenger car door for her.

TWENTY-NINE

Simon Disappears

Bob was desperate to learn more about Simon. He began to drive even more regularly to Robertsbridge and observe Louise's flat. 'This isn't stalking,' he told himself, 'This is simply an investigation'. Eventually Bob's vigilance paid off. Louise finally returned to Robertsbridge in her car two days before the trip to Chatham. Bob watched her carry her case indoors and saw the lights turn on. He waited for his rival to appear, but Louise seemed to be staying alone.

The following Sunday, Bob arrived, as usual, at about 9 am for his daily vigil. At ten o clock, he saw Simon's Mercedes arrive. He noticed that the outer door was unlocked, when Simon entered the lobby. At 10.30 am he watched Simon and Louise load their luggage into the Mercedes and leave the flat. They were closely followed by Doreen and Frank, who were on their way to the memorial to help with the decorations. Bob felt his heart beat faster as he noticed Simon kiss Louise, before shutting the passenger car door. He waited for five minutes, then drove to the back of the building. Doreen and Frank had left the front lobby door open. Bob crept inside with a piece of wire and inserted it carefully through their letter box. He wiggled it around and hooked one of the keys from their rack. It was like fishing. He wondered what he had caught. It was a single Yale key on a large ring. It fitted snugly into the lock of their ground floor flat, and he opened the door. Louise's door keys were hanging on the rack, conveniently attached to a label, which said, 'Upstairs'. He put Louise's keys in his pocket and replaced Doreen and Frank's Yale key. He carefully closed their front door and left the outer lobby door unlocked, exactly as he had found it. The outdoor congregation were watching a truck deliver a large Christmas tree to be erected next to the Memorial, ready to be blessed, as Bob drove out of the village.

Louise and Simon hadn't, as yet, decided which home they would travel to on their return from Chatham to East Sussex. They stopped for lunch just outside Ashford and began to plan the next few weeks.

"I would be more secure and organised, if I knew where I would be and when," explained Louise. "I feel a bit like a ping pong ball at the moment."

She hesitated, "Things are moving very quickly, Simon. The sensible side of me says we should take time to get to know each other better."

"How long did you take to get to know Charlie before you moved in together?" asked Simon.

"Almost three years," replied Louise.

"And did those three years help you to know him any better when you married him?"

"No, not really. I was very naïve, and hardly even knew myself."

"And are you still as naïve now?" Simon challenged her.

"Of course not."

"So maybe you don't need so much time now."

"You should have been a barrister. You argue too well!"

"I know what I want Louise and I'll fight for it. That's not the same thing as arguing."

"And once you've got what you want, will it lose its appeal?"

"That, sweetheart, is a very cruel question. I will fight to keep you. In any case, how long have I got to live? Twenty years maybe? Not long enough time for me to take you for granted."

"Simon, you are such an odd mixture of reason and romance. I'm not always sure what you are thinking."

"And you, Louise Watson, are an equally odd mixture of stability and raw emotion. You see, we are perfectly suited."

The conversation had gone on long enough without resolution. They eventually agreed to live in each other's houses in two weekly blocks. They would start at the studio, spend Christmas in Battle, and review the situation in January. In the meantime, Simon would help Louise finally to sell the bungalow, and to search for Ruby. They would aim to visit Rochester again early in 2017.

They arrived in Robertsbridge just before 4 pm, unaware that Bob was still watching from a distance, as part of his daily vigil.

The 'two-week plan' worked well for them. Each knew where they stood, and could now make arrangements for those simple domestic tasks, which could not be avoided. Simon began to meet Louise's circle of acquaintances in Robertsbridge. He was even a witness when Frank knocked on her door to confess they had lost Louise's door key. Joe and Oliver came to visit the studio. They were impressed with the views from the top of the house and they warmed to Louise. Oliver showed her considerable respect, which continued to stun his father.

Mrs Simms naturally turned to Louise for guidance, when she was in Battle. "It's so lovely to see a woman's touch in the house, Mr Ellis."

Simon was aware of the implicit sexism, but was nevertheless more than happy to delegate his domestic arrangements to Louise. He had spent all of his married life with the household decisions arranged by his (now) ex-wife. He was a very willing helper, but too set in his ways to adjust easily to a more contemporary equal sharing of responsibility.

Louise aimed to have the Fairlight bungalow on the market before Christmas. She approached Philip at Sussex Estates, and he was happy to offer her the promised discount. Louise then divided her time between making the final arrangements for the sale of the bungalow and ensuring that her first Christmas in Battle was a success. She painted three original watercolours, one each for Joe, Oliver and Simon, and for herself an outside view of the studio in Robertsbridge. She discovered that her father's share of the farm which had been left in trust to Joan was worth far more than anticipated. It seemed likely that her final inheritance from her mother would give her financial equality with Simon.

Simon bided his time. He wanted to sell his house in Battle and jointly purchase a home with Louise. He wanted to confirm their relationship in a legal contract. If Louise was willing, he would marry her. In the meantime, he spent his spare time searching the internet for more information about Ruby. Eventually, frustrated by his lack of progress and, with Louise's agreement, he paid an adoption search agency to take on the task. Louise and Simon had already decided to delay their return to Rochester until early in the new year, so there was no need to hurry.

Shortly before Christmas, Simon and Louise installed themselves back in Battle for their festive fortnight. Louise had persuaded Simon to let her take charge of decorating his house for Christmas. Louise enjoyed anything creative, but she used pleasing Sophie as an excuse. She also now had a buyer for the bungalow and an exchange of contracts was imminent, so she wanted a distraction.

"I can't believe it's almost sold," said Louise. "It's the end of an era."

"Are you sure you have taken everything you want from the bungalow, Lou? Nothing of sentimental value left? Did you recheck the loft?"

Louise admitted to Simon that she had not entered the loft since the week after the funeral, but she was sure there was nothing there. On Christmas Eve afternoon, Louise returned to Robertsbridge to drop off a few Christmas cards, collect an extra box of decorations, and grab a few more paints to add some last finishing touches to her painting for Simon. After she had left, Simon secretly took one set of the keys to Fairlight from their assigned drawer and drove to the bungalow to make a final check of the loft. He imagined how pleased Louise would be, if he discovered an extra photograph or something else of significance.

Bob had watched Louise's earlier departure from Robertsbridge. He decided that the Christmas period would be an ideal time to examine her studio in her absence. He still wondered if Joan had left any evidence of her financial dealings with him. He didn't want to give the police an excuse to search his home in Hastings. In the meantime, having spotted the 'under offer' sign on Joan's bungalow, Bob drove to Fairlight for a final look. He had not dared to break in again, since the police had been called.

When Bob arrived on Christmas Eve, it was almost dusk. Simon's car was parked outside the bungalow. The front door was ajar, and Bob pushed it open. He hobbled into the hallway. The retractable loft steps were underneath the loft hatch. Bob could see the flicker of a torch and hear Simon's feet in the attic. Simon heard the sound of uneven steps coming from the hallway and called out, "Hello. Is someone there?" Bob steadied himself on the hall table and pushed the ladder back up with all his strength towards the loft. He inhaled deeply and with one final thrust swung the hatch upwards. It automatically locked shut behind the ladder. Exhausted and in pain, Bob leaned against the wall to recover. He could hear Simon's voice calling out. The voice became fainter as Bob picked up Joan's new house keys from the hall table and hobbled towards the front entrance. He locked the door on his way out and drove straight to Robertsbridge, parking around the back of the studio. He let himself in with his newly acquired key and hobbled very slowly and painfully up the stairs.

Louise had parked in the High Street, and walked round to the Studio after delivering her cards. She noticed that the outer door was open, and assumed that Doreen had forgotten to lock it. She used her key to unlock the inner door. Unaware of any intrusion, Louise switched on the stairwell light, and climbed straight up to the studio turning on lights, as she went. Bob had no time to hide. He stood and stared at her, when she entered the studio.

"Bob, what are you doing here?"

He thought quickly.

"I had a Christmas card for you. Doreen lent me the key."

"That's nice, Bob, though I'm surprised she let you in. How on earth did you manage the stairs? Where is the card then?"

Bob moved past Louise towards the studio door, "I dropped it."

Louise became suspicious "I thought Frank said Doreen had lost my key."

Bob stepped unsteadily backwards into the upper lobby. He lost his footing and tumbled down the steep staircase. When his crumpled body reached the lower landing, it was motionless.

Louise hurried down the steps towards Bob. She knelt beside him and listened. He was breathing, but unconscious. She took the mobile phone from her pocket and dialled 999.

"Yes, he is breathing. No, he is not conscious. No, I can't see any blood. Yes, I do know him, but I think he stole the keys to my flat and let himself in." The call centre operator insisted that Louise kept the phone line open, until the ambulance arrived. She stepped over Bob, descended to the ground floor and unlocked the inner door. Eventually two paramedics let themselves in. They checked his vital signs and brought a specialist stretcher chair from the ambulance. Within half an hour, Bob was on his way to the Conquest Hospital in Hastings. Louise rang Simon's mobile, but there was no reply.

"Why don't you answer, when I need you?"

She locked the flat and drove back to Battle. The house was empty. Simon was still not answering his mobile phone. Perhaps he had gone for a drink with Joe. She mustn't appear to be too pushy. Louise decided to wait for at least two hours before contacting Joe.

Simon had not heard Bob enter the bungalow in Fairlight. He had been busy searching through the empty loft area with his torch. He heard a noise in the hallway and looked down through the hatch. He just caught a glimpse of Bob's face, before the hatch was bolted from the outside. He tried to leave the loft, but realised he was locked in. He put his hand through the metal rungs of the ladder and banged repeatedly at the heavy duty hatch, but it would not move. He searched in his pocket for his mobile phone, and realised he had left it in the car. Darkness had fallen, and the loft light wasn't working. Simon was totally reliant on his torch. He noticed the brightness was diminishing, and guessed the battery was low. He turned the torch off and on again and the light faded, before disappearing altogether. Simon's watch was backlit, but provided no more than a very faint glow. He kept pressing the button to check the time. Surely someone would miss him, but how would they know he was here? There was no window in the loft, and without a light he could see very little. His eyes did not adjust to the darkness. The floor was only partially boarded. It was almost impossible for Simon to keep his balance on the batons in the dark. He decided not to move around. He would need to wait until the morning, when he expected that a small amount of light would penetrate gaps in the tiles. At 9 pm, he made a pillow from his coat and hoped the temperature would not drop too low. He tried to sleep.

At 9 pm Louise rang Simon's mobile for a final time. It went to ansaphone. Louise rang Joe. Simon wasn't there, and Joe had not heard from him.

"I'll ring Oliver and get back to you."

By 10 pm they had contacted everyone they could think of, but without success. Joe left Caroline and Sophie at home and walked round to Simon's house.

"I'll ring the police and see if we can report Dad missing. Have you rung the hospitals?"

"I am not next of kin, Joe. No one will speak to me."

"You're on coffee duty then, while I make the calls."

No-one had any news to help them. Joe rang Caroline.

"Dad seems to have disappeared. Would you mind if I stayed here tonight, in case he makes contact. Tell Sophie I will be back early tomorrow morning. Yes, I know tomorrow is Christmas Day. I promise I will be back early."

"You might as well go to bed, Louise. I'll sleep in the spare room. We can't do anything else tonight. If you think of anything at all, write it down, and we can discuss it tomorrow morning." Louise was struck by how much Joe resembled Simon. She slept hardly at all. Her thoughts were so confused that she could make no sense of her worries. At 4 am Louise went downstairs to make coffee. She was shortly joined by Joe. "Happy Christmas, Louise."

"And to you, Joe."

"Did you sleep?"

"Not at all. You?"

"Me neither."

"What on earth are we going to do?" asked Joe.

Joe's presence helped Louise to be brave, "I have absolutely no idea."

Joe thought for a while and then said, "I want you to tell me again everything you did yesterday."

Louise retraced her steps in detail for Joe, her journey to Robertsbridge, finding Bob, the accident."

"And Dad's car isn't here, so he must have gone somewhere. Tell me everything you can about Bob. Perhaps there is a connection."

As Louise began to talk about Bob, she was struck by how much of it was odd, Bob's arrival at Fairlight after the initial break-in, the unexplained payment of £25,000, Bob's appearance at her flat yesterday. "I need to tell you something else, Joe, but I've not told your dad, so I'd rather you kept it to yourself. When I was eleven, Bob kept trying to hug me. That's why I refused to play with him any more."

"Do you mean... oh you know... touching you? Sorry, I have to ask."

"No, Joe, it wasn't abuse, just a bit over the top, creepy."

"How old was he at the time?"

"About nineteen, I think."

"Good thing you kept him at a distance. I do understand why you didn't tell Dad."

"So what should we do?"

"Do you know where Bob lives?"

"In Hastings, but he's in hospital."

"Where is his car?"

"Somewhere in Robertsbridge, I suppose."

"Come on let's go and find it. If Dad wants to make contact, he has your mobile number. It's better that we do something, anything, I think. I'll phone Caroline."

Joe walked into another room, and Louise heard muffled voices. He returned a few minutes later. "Wrap up warm, it's cold."

The early winter sun had not begun to rise, and the roads were icy. Joe climbed into Louise's car, and she drove carefully to Robertsbridge. Bob's car was parked behind her flat.

"How stupid! I never checked for his car after the ambulance left," Louise confessed.

"We'd better stay together," instructed Joe, as they climbed the stairs to the studio. Louise noticed scratches on the walls where Bob had fallen. Joe searched around Louise's flat for clues, but found nothing relevant. They returned to Bob's car and looked through the window. Joe saw an air freshener, a daily newspaper, and, on the passenger seat, an envelope from Sussex Estates. Louise stared at the envelope.

"That's the agent who is selling my mother's bungalow."

THIRTY

Simon Reappears

Joe and Louise climbed back into her car, and she started to drive to Fairlight. She turned off to Battle.

"Where are you going?" asked Joe.

"I need the bungalow house key. There are two sets in Simon's desk."

Joe rang Caroline again, while Louise found the key.

"No, of course you can't come with us. You can't leave Sophie, and she certainly can't come. Yes, I will take care, and, yes, I will look after Louise. I love you too."

Louise waited for Joe to finish.

"One set of keys to the bungalow is missing. We need to hurry."

Joe offered to drive Louise's car, but she refused. She drove as fast as she could.

They arrived at Joan's bungalow at 7.30 am. Coloured lights were flashing in the windows of neighbouring properties to welcome the start of Christmas Day. Simon's car was in the drive.

"I'm nervous Joe. What are we going to find? Should we ring the police?"

"Let's just go in. It will save time."

Joe picked up his phone. "I'm going to ring Caroline first." He keyed in his home number. "Hello darling, we're in Fairlight. We have found Dad's car. If I don't ring back in fifteen minutes,

173

ring the police. Love to Sophie," Joe finished the call quickly. Louise could only imagine the panic that Caroline must be feeling.

As they entered the bungalow, they could hear a loud banging noise. It was coming from the lounge. Joe stepped in front of Louise and they both stared into the room. A shower of plaster was falling from a hole in the ceiling. There was a loud crack, and Simon's feet appeared through the hole. Joe rushed towards his father and helped to steady the rest of his body as it dropped towards the lounge floor. They both fell in slow motion on to the patterned carpet. Simon's hair was full of dust. Father and son sat up together apparently unharmed. Simon wiped the debris from his face and spoke, "You two took your time."

Louise burst into tears, "We didn't know where you were."

"Some bloke locked me in the loft. I hope he's gone."

"Oh yes, he's gone," uttered Louise through her sobs.

"How can you be sure?" asked Simon.

"We're sure," laughed Joe, "Because he's in hospital. Your nutty girlfriend frightened him so much that he fell down the stairs. Happy Christmas, Dad!"

There was no milk in the bungalow, so Louise made three black coffees, while Joe rang Caroline. Simon went out to his car, found his phone, and rang the police.

"They have agreed to interview us later today in Battle."

Simon gave Joe his car keys, and Louise drove Simon back to Battle. By lunchtime they were all sitting round the Christmas dinner table at Joe and Caroline's. The police phoned during the afternoon to say they would be round in the evening on Christmas Day to interview Simon and Louise. Apparently, Bob was still unconscious, but, as a precaution, the police had put him under arrest with a police guard, pending further investigations. Christmas would delay matters, but they would obtain a search warrant for Bob's house as soon as possible.

"Better bake more mince pies, Caroline," chuckled Joe. "We have extra visitors on the way."

By the time Oliver arrived, Simon and Louise were sat by the Christmas tree being interviewed by CID.

"I knew she was trouble," remarked Olivier amiably looking towards Louise.

"From what you have told us," explained the police, "We do think he might be dangerous. Now there is stalking legislation in place, we have more options to detain him. While he is unconscious, he is no risk, but it also means we can't interview him. We just want to advise you to take reasonable precautions for your safety. Try to stay together. No more secret excursions to lofts."

The police took the spare set of keys to Joan's bungalow so they could organise a forensic examination of the loft hatch. They also asked Louise if they could interview her at Robertsbridge, just in case Bob claimed that Louise had pushed him down the stairs.

"You are not to worry about this, Mrs Watson. The hospital staff have said his injuries indicated a fall, and we already have a lot of evidence against him."

Once the police had left, Joe poured everyone a large drink, and Sophie persuaded Louise to play a game of her new giant Jenga. When the blocks crashed to the floor, Simon glanced at Sophie.

"You've chosen the right game, Sophie, Louise is an expert at sending things tumbling."

"Well at least I don't make holes in people's ceilings," retorted Louise.

"What on earth are you two going to do with yourselves when this is over? Your lives will seem very dull," added Joe.

"Suddenly the word 'dull' is very appealing, Joe," observed Louise.

Once it was after Sophie's bedtime, Simon and Louise walked back to Simon's house. A Christmas chill added sparkle to the pavements. They could see a couple sitting together through the window of one of the houses in Simon's road.

"Maybe next year that will be us," said Simon hopefully.

"I seriously thought I might have frightened you off," admitted Louise.

"Oh no, you've totally trapped me. I am obliged to stay with you now. You are not safe to be left alone."

"How on earth did you stay warm in the loft overnight?"

"It was bloody freezing, Lou. I kept moving my legs to try and keep my circulation going. It was lucky you'd left the heating on low. That probably saved me from hypothermia. I didn't want to make a big deal of it in front of Sophie, but I was very scared. I thought Bob might come back, though of course, I didn't know it was Bob. As soon as the morning light began to appear through the roof tiles. I started to make a hole in the floor. I used one of the roof batons. I'm sorry about the damage, Louise."

"As if I care about that. I feel so guilty. If I had been more suspicious of Bob, this might have been avoided."

"This is not your fault, Lou. I should never have gone to the bungalow alone. I was trying to be a hero."

When they arrived home, Simon made them each a cup of hot chocolate. "I know it's Christmas Day, but I'm going to turn in. I think I've had enough excitement today. Come up whenever you want." He was yawning.

Louise finished her drink and climbed the stairs. She couldn't settle, but she needed to sleep. Simon was already in bed with his eyes closed. She changed into her nightwear quietly and crept into bed beside him. She could feel the rhythm of his breathing. She needed to feel him close and gently touched his back.

"Happy Christmas, sweetheart," he mumbled.

She started to draw pictures on his back with her finger.

"That feels good Are you trying to seduce me?"

"Maybe," giggled Louise.

"Should I play 'hard to get'?"

"If you like."

"I don't like."

Simon turned round and slipped both hands underneath her pyjamas. He brushed her ear and neck with his lips. He kissed her repeatedly with passion so that his fingers could travel with ease through her body. Louise responded and twisted her long legs to surround his hips. She stroked him with her mouth until his arousal was irrepressible. When their bodies finally reached a mutual climax, they felt the tension of the day drift away. They fell into an immediate and much needed sleep.

On Boxing Day, they walked into Battle and watched the gathering of the hounds and horses. The Fox Hunting ban had not prevented the annual spectacle of red coats and hunting horns, with a small group of protesters holding placards at a distance.

"You've lived in Sussex all your life. Do you approve of fox hunting?" asked Louise.

"Of course not, it's cruel," Simon replied.

Louise was relieved, and it suddenly occurred to her that she knew nothing about his political views. She doubted they would be extreme, but decided that particular conversation could wait for another occasion.

Later that day, Simon sat on his sofa and turned on the TV. Louise came and sat beside him. She lay down on the sofa and rested her head on his lap. Her legs stuck out over the edge. "You need a longer sofa."

Simon loved the way Louise showed him so much spontaneous affection. It made him feel wanted. He rested his hand on her chest.

"Lou? Can I ask you something?"

"You know you can."

"You did say, didn't you, that you only ever slept with Charlie up to your marriage. I just wondered were there others later on? I wouldn't mind, you know."

"There was no one else, Simon. I'm sorry I'm so inexperienced."

"But that's the point. You're not… inexperienced, I mean. Sometimes I worry I'll let you down. I'm not getting any younger."

"Look, Charlie was older than me, and he had loads of women before me. In the early days of our relationship, he, well you know, showed me things. Once the novelty wore off, he became very self-centred. I love the way you seem to understand my body. You know how to arouse me. I'm enjoying it. And I know we're not getting any younger. Let's just appreciate exploring each other while we can, but no pressure? You have nothing to prove, Simon."

Simon lay his hand on the bare flesh of her waist. He was surprised when she didn't respond. He looked down and realised she was fast asleep.

Three days later, the police phoned Louise to inform her that Bob had regained consciousness. They planned to interview him in the next few days. In the meantime, they wanted an appointment with Louise at her studio. They gave no reason why, but requested that Simon should be present.

And so it was that in early January 2017, Louise and Simon found themselves nervously seated in her studio in the company of a plain-clothed officer and a female constable.

"We have been into Robert Gresham's' house, and found some disturbing material. On the basis of this, we will be opposing bail. We will recommend that he is kept in custody until his trial. Have you ever been to his house?"

"No, no-one was invited, not even my mum, who gave him lunch every week."

"He appears to have been obsessed with you, Mrs Watson. When did you first meet him?"

"When I was three, I think."

"And did he ever try to… assault you… sexually, I mean?"

"When I was eleven, he began to try and hug me a lot. It was not assault. Well, I didn't see it that way, but I told my mum I didn't want him round any more, when I was on my own."

"I'm sorry, Mrs Watson, but I have to ask. Did he ever ask you to remove clothing or touch you in intimate places?"

"Certainly not. I wouldn't have let him. As I grew older, when he tried to hug me, I didn't like it and ran off."

"It sounds like you had a very sensible upbringing, and instinctively knew how to protect yourself. Nevertheless, we will need to arrange a specialist interview with a trained female officer. In the meantime, I have some photos to show you. I should warn you that they are distressing. This is a room in Robert Gresham's house."

The officer produced several photos of a large pinboard on the wall in a room in Bob's house. It was filled with photos of Louise taken ever since she split up with Charlie. Bob's own photo was also on the wall next to Louise. More worrying was a very recent photo taken at a distance of Louise and Simon. Simon's face was scribbled out with black felt pen.

"We also found several scrap books full of photographs of you as a child, and as a young adult."

"This feels like a crime drama," observed Louise.

"It feels bloody perverted to me," interjected Simon, "I hope you're going to lock him up!"

"Well, TV crimes are based on true cases, even if they are often exaggerated, Mrs Watson. The problem with stalking behaviour is that it can suddenly escalate. Robert Gresham appears to have become much more desperate recently."

"What about the £25,000?" asked Simon "Have you found out anything about that?"

"When Robert Gresham is fit enough for a longer interview, we will pursue the matter further. In the meantime, we do have a theory about the money, but need more evidence. Ring me in a couple of weeks, can you?" The police officer passed Simon a card.

THIRTY-ONE

Making Plans

Simon and Louise spent all of January sorting out Joan's bungalow. The earlier buyer had refused to wait for the repairs to the lounge ceiling and pulled out. Philip suspected that they had been put off by the police involvement. However, a new buyer came forward quickly, and Simon accompanied Louise to Philip's office in Hastings. She signed the contract, which had been faxed through from the buyer's solicitor.

It was the first time that Simon had met Philip, and the estate agent made a point of telling Simon he had supervised the sale personally.

"I'm sure Louise is very grateful," responded Simon, trying to avoid sarcasm.

"Yes, you've been very helpful, thank you, Philip," added Louise.

Contracts were exchanged a week later, and Louise arranged for the removal of the final items of furniture. When the sale was completed, Louise called Simon to look at her online bank statement on her laptop.

"I don't believe I have all this money."

Simon kissed her, "I love you even more now."

"I feel as if we have finally achieved something," confessed Louise. She had also secretly asked an estate agent in Robertsbridge to look round the studio, and had been surprised at the high valuation. Until now the pressure to make a joint purchase with Simon had all come from Simon, but Louise was beginning to feel ready to make the commitment. Although far more imaginative than Simon, Louise still struggled to envisage what their shared home might look like, but she was ready to begin the conversation.

They were both staying in Battle when she broached the subject. It was a cold mid-February morning, and Simon was sitting at his kitchen table opening his post. Louise touched his hand and he looked up.

"Are you very attached to this house?"

Simon set aside the letters and gave her a quizzical look.

"Why the question?"

"I just wondered whether we should consider buying somewhere together?"

"Would you sell the studio?"

"I had it valued last week."

"That was sneaky. Did you use Philip?"

"No, a local agent in Robertsbridge."

Simon stood up and beckoned Louise into his arms.

"I wasn't sure whether you would be able to separate yourself from the past."

"I need to move on, Simon. That is, if it's what you want."

"It is exactly what I want."

They cooked some breakfast together, as if needing to consolidate their decision with routine. Even in moments of extreme tension, they had rarely argued over domestic arrangements. Louise pointed this out to Simon.

"That's because I'm so easy going," Simon smiled.

Louise rolled her eyes, "Where would we live?"

"I'd rather not move too far from Joe... and Oliver of course, though he won't stay in Ninfield forever. Is that a problem?"

"It's fine. I don't really have ties to any location. I will miss the studio though. I'd like a room where I can paint."

"You can have a freezing cold shed in the garden," Simon grinned. "Actually, Lou, one of the things I really like about your studio, is the way your painting merges into the living space. It makes me feel involved. I don't like the idea of losing you to a workshop or an outhouse."

"I never thought about it that way, but you're right. I moved half my kitchen into the studio. I very rarely used the lower floor. Mind you, it was partly because of the view. There's so much to think about, Simon."

"It'll be fun looking around, planning our future together." Simon absent-mindedly picked up the post as he spoke. He opened one of the envelopes, and read the contents, "And now we have something else to think about." He looked up at Louise, "The agency have traced Ruby."

THIRTY-TWO

Martha

Martha Willis had always been poor. She had received a poor education, was brought up in poor quality housing, and was loved by poor parents with a poor income. Consequently, she had poor expectations for herself. She left school at fourteen and found a job in a clothing factory, where the women earned even less than the men. Dissatisfaction with the monotony of her work as a machinist led her to apply for a post in a residential home. By the time she was twenty, she had changed her career from manufacturing to caring. She developed into a poorly paid, but experienced and well respected care assistant, working in a home for adults with severe learning needs, including those suffering from early onset dementia.

Martha had an absent husband, two grown up children, and three grandchildren, all of whom relied on her from time to time to subsidise their need for shoes or payment for school trips. The family view that Martha had very little purpose for her own money disregarded Martha's need to pay her own rent and purchase food. Nevertheless, Martha regularly helped out her family financially and took pleasure in doing so.

As well as being a care assistant, Martha was later asked to take the role of 'Activities Co-ordinator' within the home. She organised gardening clubs, entertainment and craft sessions for the residents. She was always surprised by the skills of people who could barely remember their own name. The residents loved Martha and wanted to please her. She was not allowed to accept financial gifts, but did occasionally accept a present of an activity-club-grown plant or a painting. Most were then discarded privately, but Martha had kept her very first gift, a watercolour, which she had framed and hung on her living room wall. It was a remarkable portrayal of an adult and young child walking hand in hand in a park. Cathy had asked Martha to write the words 'Lou Lou' on the back of the painting. Martha often peered deeply into the depths of the picture and wondered how much of her past Cathy had remembered when she painted the scene.

Cathy was admitted to 'Three Trees' Residential Care Home in the Summer of 1958. It was an unenlightened time for mental health patients. They were locked up and often sedated. Anxiety was regularly confused with aggression. Cathy had made many escape attempts in her first year, sometimes successfully. She was twice found watching the playground at a local infant school. In an attempt to keep her in the home, the staff often tethered her arms to her chair. When twenty-year-old Martha arrived in 1960, she took an interest in Martha and started to chat with her.

"How are you today, Cathy?"

"I am fine, I am waiting for Lou Lou. When I go home, we will make cakes and decorate them with pink icing."

"Do you like making cakes, Cathy?"

"I like decorating them with icing."

"Shall we make some cakes together?"

And Martha started a cooking session for two of the residents. It was an unusual move, but the nurse in charge noticed that it calmed down the participants. They needed less sedation.

"Your icing is beautiful, Cathy. Do you like art?"

"I have a paintbrush and paper and I make pictures for Lou Lou."

So Martha used her own money to buy a set of brushes and a small watercolour pallet for Cathy. The staff were astounded at the artwork which Cathy produced. Her paintings were framed and hung on the care home walls.

When Cathy's condition deteriorated, she was no longer able to control a paintbrush. She grew restless and kept trying to grab the other residents and move their possessions. In desperation Martha purchased a baby doll and gave it to Cathy to hold. The transformation was instant. Cathy hugged the doll and silently rocked in her chair.

"We are together now, Lou Lou. No one will take you from me. I will protect you always."

When Cathy died in 1970, no family could be found to attend the funeral. Cathy's admission records had indicated a connection with the Sisters of Mercy in Chatham, so Cathy's body was passed into their care. Martha represented the care home at the short convent funeral. At Martha's request, the baby doll was put inside the coffin and laid to rest with Cathy.

"I hope that baby Lou Lou will comfort you always," Martha wept the silent words, as the coffin was lowered in to the grave.

THIRTY-THREE

Finding Ruby

Heritage Adoption Investigation Services,
Kingsgate,
Crawley,
RH10 1EN

10th February 2017
Dear Mr Ellis,
I am writing to inform you that we have located a Ruby
Eldridge (nee Makepiece) with a date of birth within your
specified range. She is a resident of a care home in the Midlands.
Our initial enquiries indicate that she is of sound mind and
does have some information which is relevant to Mrs Watson's
search. If you wish to meet her, we will request permission from
the care home, and send you contact details. The lady concerned
is quite frail, so we would advise you not to delay your visit
unduly.
We enclose our final account.
Kind regards,
A Miller
Senior Investigator

Louise went pale, "I suppose we have to do this."
"It's your choice, Louise."

"I hear the Midlands are very nice in February."

"And my car could do with a long run. Do you want me to reply?"

"Please, Simon. Let's get this over as soon as possible."

Simon paid the bill by bank transfer and telephoned the investigation agency to ask them to proceed. The agency contacted him two hours later to say they had permission from the care home. They gave him the name of the home and contact details. The home responded quickly to his call, and said that Louise and Simon could turn up any afternoon the following week. Louise booked a room for herself and Simon in a nearby hotel for two nights.

The following Monday, Louise and Simon set off in Simon's Mercedes heading through the Dartford Tunnel to Northampton. They passed the time by describing their ideal home to each other. As the journey progressed, their conversation began to get silly. By the time they reached the hotel, they had settled on an open plan art studio/living area with two lifts, close to Joe's, with remote integral night lights, magnificent sea views and no loft.

The hotel room was on the fourth floor.

"Sorry, it isn't a suite. I thought we should save our pennies for the house move."

"As long as it has a very large duvet, and extra blankets, I won't complain," joked Simon.

They rang the care home to say they would be there at 2 pm the following day.

"This lady," said Louise to Simon at the hotel, "Eighty-two-year-old Ruby, used to have my grandma's surname, so she might be a blood relative."

"Or just as likely, she could be the offspring of someone who married a blood relative with the surname Makepiece. It's very complicated. I sincerely hope she is 'with it' enough to help us."

They drove to the home, parked in the car park and rang the doorbell of the impressive entrance. They were asked to sign in at a well-appointed reception area. The entire establishment was immaculately clean, but every now and then a faint smell of toilets wafted through the air. Louise looked nervously at Simon.

"Ruby is waiting for you in the visitor's day room. I think you'll like her. She is very chatty. She has been talking about you all morning." The uniformed carer led the way.

"A small, smartly-dressed, grey-haired lady was sitting in a lightly-upholstered upright chair. She watched Louise and Simon enter the room.

"I can't get up. My legs don't work." Ruby's face changed to a more positive expression, "You are Louise, I know you are Louise. You still have that lovely blonde hair, but I bet it's out of a bottle these days. How old are you?" The words fell out of Ruby's mouth without pausing for breath.

"I'm sixty-one."

"And you are still beautiful. Is this your young man?"

Simon gave Ruby his hand, "Yes, Ruby. My name is Simon."

He moved two chairs, so they could form a small circle. Ruby rang a bell. "They'll come quickly today, because you're here. A carer appeared.

"Tea for three please. And cake… you want cake?" Louise nodded. "Cake, as well, please. Some of the residents here have lost their marbles, but I've still got mine, and I won't be treated like an idiot. So… this is wonderful. I have always wanted to know what happened to you, and just to look at you. And here you are, tall and beautiful with a fine young man. I want to know everything that you have been doing."

Louise and Simon suddenly realised that Ruby was as hungry for information as they were. Simon interrupted, "Ruby, before Louise gives you her life story, we really need some information. How did Louise's mother die, and what happened to her grandma?"

Ruby went pale, "You don't know? No one told you?"

"I don't know anything, Ruby, about my life before the age of three."

"You'll need more than tea. I should have ordered you a stiff drink."

The tea arrived, and Ruby became diverted. She insisted on pouring it into the cups for everyone with her trembling hand. "This is Louise," she said to the carer. She is my cousin's granddaughter. Simon whispered to Louise, "We might need several days."

"I hope you are feeling strong," said Ruby "You are in for a shock."

"Just tell me," Louise instructed Ruby.

"Your mother was fifteen…"

"Patricia?" interrupted Louise.

"Yes, Patricia. She was fifteen and on her way home from school, from art club. She was very good at art, like her mother." Simon squeezed Louise's hand.

"It was dark, late October. The clocks had gone back. Patricia was attacked and raped in a Rochester churchyard. She slowly recovered, but three months later your mother discovered she was pregnant."

Louise gasped.

"Are you alright?" asked Simon, "It's a lot to take in."

Louise was trembling, "I'm fine."

Ruby continued "You have to remember that this was the fifties. Babies born out of wedlock were considered shameful. Rape or no rape, your mother's pregnancy was kept a secret."

"Did they catch the man who raped her?"

"No, he was never caught."

"So my real father, the rapist, never knew about me. I think I am pleased that he didn't know."

"Your mother, Patricia, was sent to the convent in Chatham to give birth. She was there for five weeks. Cathy, your grandma, was not allowed to visit Patricia at the convent. You were to be adopted."

"What happened?"

"Patricia died in childbirth. I remember that there was a link to the attack, a possible brain haemorrhage. Cathy wasn't told for three days. Those nuns were monsters, even worse than my prison officers here. When Cathy found out, she went to the convent and demanded to take you home." Louise noticed that Simon was taking notes.

"Cathy was a wealthy widow, so I used to go and stay to keep her company. I was just a poor cousin. Donald, your uncle, would have been your grandpa, but he died in the war. He was a pilot. I lived in Dartford with my seven younger brothers and sisters. Then Cathy invited me to stay from time to time and help with the baby… with you. We visited Patricia's grave one time, but we were never allowed in again."

Louise noticed that Ruby was looking tired. "Shall we come back tomorrow, Ruby? You can tell me the rest then."

"Lovely. Can you bring me a bottle of whisky and some decent biscuits?"

"We certainly can, Ruby," Simon chuckled.

"And tomorrow, you must tell me everything about yourself."

"Ruby, can I ask you one more question before I go?"

"Of course."

"What happened to my grandmother, to Nana?"

"Nana, oh yes, you called her 'Nana'. She began to lose her marbles, like most of this lot in here. I was away when they took you to the children's home. I wanted to keep you, but with seven brothers and sisters, it wasn't an option."

Ruby's eyes were closing.

"One final question," said Simon "What sort of biscuits?"

"Bourbons," Ruby replied, and she drifted off to sleep.

Simon drove Louise back to the hotel. They stayed silent until they reached their room. Simon stood in the window and looked at Louise. She was staring into space.

"Speak to me, Lou"

"I am the daughter of a rapist."

"You are, and you have just met your first blood relation who is alive, and she is quite delightful."

"She is, isn't she? Can we be sure she is a blood relative?"

"Yes, I've been working it out from what she said. Her father must have been your grandfather's much younger and, apparently much poorer, brother. She was born a Makepiece… as you were. And your grandfather was a WW2 Pilot. What's one rapist amongst all that glory?"

"You are amazing, Simon, you have made me feel better

already… 'my young man'." Louise giggled, "I think we should add some flowers to the whisky and the bourbons."

They rested in the hotel and then walked into the town centre for an evening meal. As they sat eating, Louise would blurt out sudden thoughts.

"I keep wondering how Patricia was treated by the nuns."

"You can't change the past, Louise. You should only worry about what you can change. Cathy would have been so proud of you… of your paintings."

"I should paint something for Ruby. So many unanswered questions! The dark, I must ask about my fear of the dark!"

"Write down your questions, Lou. Your mind must be overflowing, but don't expect to get answers to everything. Why did you say you were pleased that the attacker, the rapist never knew about you?"

"Because it somehow makes him anonymous. I don't want to have to think about him or try to understand him. I can just forget he existed."

They walked back to the hotel, hand in hand. Louise expected a disturbed night, but her sleep was dreamless.

Their trip to the care home the following afternoon was far more relaxed. They had wandered into Northampton town centre in the morning and bought two bottles of malt whisky, five large packets of bourbons and a bouquet of flowers.

"Do you think Ruby is allowed alcohol?"

"Does it matter?"

"No, not really, but let's put the bottles in a bag, just in case."

Ruby was waiting for them with tea already set out on a tray. Simon suspected that she kept her carers well under control. Ruby told Louise how she had been rescued from the darkness in the house in Penhurst Crescent by a young police constable. Louise told Ruby about Joan and Peter, her teaching career, her painting, and how she had met Simon. Ruby explained that she had married well, was now widowed, and was sometimes visited by her children and grandchildren. The conversation was joyful.

"More blood relatives," murmured Simon. He had a book

full of notes of names of people and places which he would piece together when they returned home.

At exactly the same time as the day before, Ruby began to drift into a sleep, and Louise and Simon crept away. They asked the carer to inform Ruby that they would visit again in a few weeks' time.

Simon turned to Louise in the car park, "Louise Makepiece, Windsor, Watson, and all your component parts, you are an impressive woman from an impressive family."

"With an even more impressive young man."

THIRTY-FOUR

Moving On

L ouise's nightmares diminished after her visit to Northampton, but her need for a nightlight continued. Simon searched accessible police records but could find nothing there about Patricia's rape or Louise's transfer to the children's home. He did, however, discover a short newspaper article in the archives of the Rochester News about an attack on a young girl in 1954 in the local graveyard. At some time in the future, he would ask Louise if she wanted to pay a visit to the graveyard in Rochester, maybe in a few years' time. He contacted Rochester Grammar and obtained a whole school photo from 1954. They couldn't be sure which of the teenage faces in the lines of gymslips was Patricia, but Louise liked to scrutinise the photo and guess who her mother was. They made two more whisky laden visits to the Care Home in Northampton, before Ruby died. On the second visit Ruby suddenly remembered the name of the home in Kent in which Cathy was installed. Simon wrote it down.

Louise and Simon began to look at properties together. They had sufficient funds from Joan's estate and from the sale of Simon's business to make the purchase, so there was no pressure to sell Louise's flat or Simon's house in a hurry. Louise was, however, disappointed when the occasional nightmare began to return. She would also worry constantly that Simon would leave her. She would find herself in tears when she thought about it. She didn't want to expose more of her insecurities, so, unbeknown to Simon, Louise paid for some more sessions with a counsellor. She would disappear for over an hour every Wednesday afternoon and tell Simon she was going shopping.

"Why are you here, Louise?" asked the counsellor.

"Because I need to rationalise events from my past. I get nightmares. And I have met a wonderful man. I am frightened he will leave me. Things are going so well. We are buying a house together and we haven't even had a major argument."

Over several sessions, Louise told the counsellor about everything that had happened.

"So, if you did have an argument, would your relationship suffer?"

"I very much doubt it."

Ironically, it was the counselling which actually caused their first major dispute. Simon began to get suspicious about Louise's disappearance every Wednesday. He had noticed that she drove to her destination when they were in Battle, but she left on foot when in Robertsbridge. One day, he followed her at a distance as she walked down the High Street. He watched her knock on the door of a private house and emerge forty minutes later. That evening he confronted her.

He had allowed the anxiety to build up inside himself, and it was turning to anger.

"Where did you go this afternoon, Louise?"

She missed the signs of anger, and gave a flippant response.

"Clothes shopping, did you want to come with me?"

"Show me what you bought then."

It was a challenge, not a question.

Louise began to feel nervous.

"I didn't buy anything. I just looked."

Simon raised his voice.

"You didn't buy anything, because you didn't go shopping. I watched you go into a house on the High Street."

"You followed me!"

"What were you doing, Louise?"

"You don't own me, Simon. I have a right to some privacy."

"That's what Julie said, when she was having an affair."

Louise just glared at Simon, "For god's sake Simon, I'm the one who's supposed to be insecure!"

"What were you doing, Louise?"

She felt under attack. She wanted to escape. She walked into the bedroom to get away from him. He poured himself a drink, and tried to calm down. Louise sat in silence for several minutes, before returning to the studio.

"Did you really think I was having an affair?"

"You lied to me. You weren't shopping."

Louise found herself shaking and fumbled through her handbag. She found the small white card with the counsellor's name and contact details. She put it on the table in front of Simon. He picked up the card.

"I've been having weekly counselling sessions. I thought it might help with the nightmares."

"Why didn't you just tell me?"

"I didn't want to admit I needed help. I wanted you to think I was coping."

She began to feel tearful.

Simon was overwhelmed with contrition. His anger disappeared far more quickly than it had started, "Louise, darling, you are coping brilliantly. But you've been through so much. You are bound to have some symptoms of anxiety. I think counselling is an excellent idea. I just wish you had told me."

"Did you really think I was being unfaithful to you?"

Simon looked ashamed, "I did wonder."

"You're not being rational Simon. I am devoted to you. We're trying to buy a house together. In any case I wouldn't have the energy!"

"I'm sorry, but you did lie to me."

She stroked his hair.

"You mean like you lied to me, when you paid that first visit to Karen and Michael. Try to trust me. I trust you. Perhaps you should have the counselling."

Louise spoke softly to diffuse any remaining anger, "I won't deceive you again. I promise."

They clung to each other pleased to have survived the argument.

Simon suddenly returned to playfulness, "No energy for an affair? Am I really such a stud that I wear you out?"

"It has been known, but I rather like it."

The following week Louise's counsellor asked, "What are Simon's faults?"

"He's very single minded. Once he is focussed on a project, he is like a juggernaut lorry," Louise didn't want to talk about their argument.

"And if you ask him, does he slow down?"

"Always."

"Louise, I'm not supposed to give advice, but in your case, I am going to make an exception. You have been through so much that I think you can't accept when things are finally going well. Just enjoy your new life."

"And the nightmares?"

"They are lodged very deep in your past. You may have to accept them as a permanent part of your existence."

"I think I knew that really."

Louise decided she had no more need of counselling.

Simon successfully searched for 'Three Trees' home in Kent, which Ruby had mentioned. He wrote to the home to see if they had details of a Catherine Makepiece. They confirmed the date of Catherine's death, and invited Simon and Louise to visit. They travelled to Kent for a half day in the summer of 2017. It was now a local day centre for people with learning difficulties with attached sheltered accommodation. However, it had kept the name 'Three Trees'. Louise and Simon were shown into the day room by the supervisor. Three carers were sitting with the clients helping them to put together the pieces of a jigsaw and to construct simple models with boxes and glue. Louise found herself looking at a large painting on the wall. She walked over to it.

"It's good, isn't it?" said the supervisor. "When we took over ten years ago, most of the furnishings and pictures from the Care Home were destroyed, but we really liked this one, and it clearly shows the three trees in the front of the house, after which the building was named."

Louise examined the painting and called to Simon.

"Look."

In the bottom right hand corner of the painting were written the words 'Catherine Makepiece'.

"That's my grandma's name."

"How amazing! Would you like a cup of tea?" asked the supervisor.

"You do realise that we are now only a Day Centre. 'Three Trees Care Home' closed over ten years ago. I'm pretty sure all the detailed records of former residents were destroyed. We only have the register of former residents with their full names and dates of birth and death. It's very unlikely that we will have any new information for you."

"What about the staff?"

"Most of the staff left, when the was home closed."

Louise sighed, "Well at least I've seen the picture."

"It's very well painted, isn't it. We find that people with memory loss often retain quite complex skills well into their condition. Do you like painting?"

Simon interrupted. "Louise could have painted that picture. Her style is very similar."

"Well feel free to stay and finish your tea." Louise sensed that they were being moved on.

"I'll just have a word with Andrea. I believe she was a cleaner here in the Care Home Days. She works in our kitchen now." Andrea came out and spoke to them.

"I don't remember your Nan, but I do know a lady who used to work here as a carer, when it was a care home. If you give me your Nanny's name, I'll ask her if she remembers anything. Let me have your phone number. If I discover anything, I'll contact you."

Louise and Simon thanked Andrea, and left.

"I wondered if you wanted the painting," said Simon.

"I did think about it, but it belongs at 'Three Trees', doesn't it? I found that visit quite hard work."

Simon agreed, "It was hard work. They had a job to do, and weren't really interested in us. Do you think Andrea will ring us?"

"I very much doubt it."

Andrea did not ring. However, three days later they received an unexpected call from a lady named Martha.

"Is that Louise Makepiece?"

"I was known by the name of Louise Makepiece until I was three."

"My name is Martha. Andrea gave me your number. I used to work at 'Three Trees' Care Home. I knew your grandmother."

"Wow! Thank you so much for ringing me. You are the first person I've spoken to, apart from Ruby, who actually knew her. This is amazing." Louise signalled to Simon that the call was significant. He came and stood beside her and listened.

"I looked after Cathy from two years after she was admitted, until she passed away. I loved her like my own family. I have so much to tell you about her."

Martha invited Louise and Simon to her home.

Once again, they journeyed to Kent, staying this time in Rochester. They revisited Penhurst Crescent, and Hellingham House. However, neither of them suggested a visit to the churchyard. They seemed to have a silent pact that they were not yet ready. On the appointed day, Louise and Simon found Martha's house. It was an unimposing housing association end terrace on the outskirts of Rochester. Louise rang the bell, and Martha answered straight away.

"You have the look of your grandma."

Martha showed them into her front room and nervously offered tea.

Suddenly Louise went rigid. "You have one of my watercolours on your wall!"

"That's not yours. Cathy painted it."

And Louise realised that this painting, with a style so like her own, had been painted by her grandmother. The swirling image of a tree-filled park also contained an adult and a child. The child looked like the image of Louise outside Hellingham House.

"I have so much to tell you," said Martha.

Simon and Louise sat quietly ready to listen.

"Cathy was very distressed, when she was first admitted to 'Three Trees'. When I was appointed, she had been there for over two years, and was still often sedated. She was frequently agitated and strapped into a chair. She mentioned your name constantly, but was obviously no longer capable of looking after a young child. As I got to know Cathy better, I noticed she was very creative. I set up an art workshop, and it had an amazingly calming effect on her. The picture on my wall is one of the first she ever painted. I thought it was so good, and she gave it to me as a present. Cathy painted a lot in the home, before she really deteriorated. She was very young to have memory loss, but the doctors suspected that the trauma of Patricia's death, and not being allowed to grieve had brought on her early onset dementia. We weren't supposed to accept gifts from residents, but Cathy insisted that I took the painting. I had it framed. You must take it home with you Louise. I want you to have it. The painting belongs to you."

And Martha explained more to Louise about the art classes in the home, and about her nana's obsession with the baby doll. She insisted that Louise be given the painting to take home.

"Do you know where Nana is buried?" asked Louise.

"If I remember rightly, she is buried at the convent in Chatham with Patricia. I went to her funeral to represent 'Three Trees'."

They shared memories and history for over two hours, until Louise felt that they had taken up enough of Martha's time.

"Thank you for being so kind to my grandma. I feel better knowing that you were there for her."

Simon noticed that both women were fighting back their tears. As he carried the painting to his car, he turned to Louise. "Looks like we have yet another painting for our new home."

THIRTY-FIVE

A wedding in Brighton

Bob finally admitted to the police that he had persuaded Joan to pay him £25,000 in return for his silence about Louise's adoption.

"That is really wicked," declared Louise, "He knew Mum was dying. That is just extortion." She could barely contain her anger, "I'd like to… how could he be so vile?"

The money was eventually returned to Joan's estate. Bob received a five-year sentence for stalking, and a permanent court order to keep his distance from Simon and Louise. Simon was seriously worried that Bob might return to his old ways, when eventually released, but the police pointed out that, if he survived his stretch in jail, Bob would be well into his seventies by the end of his prison term. His mobility was deteriorating, and it was likely he would end up in a care home.

Ever since the incident at the studio, Louise had refused to stay there alone, so, although in theory they still stuck to the two-week plan, they tended to extend their stays in Battle and spend shorter periods in Robertsbridge. Simon would always accompany Louise to the studio when she collected her post and checked the ansaphone. Nevertheless, Louise and Simon began to feel more secure with each other and learned to talk through their concerns.

"You know what worries me most?" Louise admitted to Simon, "That early dementia is hereditary. That one day you will find me wandering around Robertsbridge, not knowing where I live."

Simon laughed out loud. "Cathy was a lot younger than you, when she lost it, and Martha did say that it may have been caused by trauma. In any case you are one of the most alert people I know. I am far more forgetful than you."

"Promise me that you'll tell me, if you notice any signs."

"I promise. And you have forgotten that you offered me a coffee."

Louise's face fell. "I don't remember that."

Simon chuckled. "I was teasing you. I made it up. I just wanted a coffee." He stood up and made them both a drink. They sat at the studio table drinking coffee, while Louise sifted through the junk mail to see if there were any letters worth reading. She opened an embossed, multi-coloured envelope and read the contents. "We've been invited to a wedding."

"Whose?"

"Gillian and Catherine. They are getting married at The Royal Victoria in Brighton."

"Wow!"

"The last time I went to The Royal Victoria was when my parents met Mandy and Stewart. Mandy bought a cashmere twinset especially for the occasion."

"Please promise me you won't buy a cashmere twinset."

Louise laughed, "I promise. It will be the first wedding we have been invited to as a proper couple."

"As opposed to an improper couple. I'm pleased they have invited us."

"I expect Michelle will be there."

"After all we've been through, I think we can cope with Michelle," responded Simon.

"She's still very attractive. You'll like her."

"No-one compares with you, Louise."

"Flatterer!"

The day of the wedding arrived quickly.

Louise had bought an expensive new floaty outfit and

banished Simon to the spare bedroom in Battle, while she got ready. Simon changed into his suit, while Louise was dressing. When she came downstairs he was sitting, suited, waiting for her to appear. He stood up to admire her. Louise just stared at him.

"Is something wrong?"

"It's the first time I've seen you wear a suit, Simon. You look amazing."

"I used to wear a suit every day for work, but you get out of the habit. Actually, this tie is very uncomfortable."

Simon drove Louise to Brighton and pulled up on the seafront outside the Royal Victoria Hotel. He handed his keys to the concierge, and they walked into the imposing lobby area. A porter showed them to the wedding suite. A crystal chandelier shot arcs of coloured light across the ceiling, and seventy beautifully upholstered chairs were laid out in lines. The room was already half full. Eyes turned as Louise and Simon entered. Even in their sixties, their good looks effortlessly commanded attention.

"Who are all these people?" Simon asked.

"Work colleagues and friends, I suppose… and a few family members. Michelle is over there with her third husband. Come on, I'll introduce you."

They walked over to Michelle. "How are you? This is Simon."

"And this is Anthony."

The men shook hands, and Simon and Louise returned to their seats. "I'm glad that's over. He looks quite nice, her latest bloke. And you were wrong about Michelle. I don't fancy her… too… fluffy."

A side door opened, and the registrar entered the room with her assistant. They stood behind the ornate rectangular table. Then the wide double doors opened at the rear of the suite. A single flute began to play Pachelbel's Canon, and the couple walked down the central aisle. Simon had not yet met Gillian, so he turned in curiosity. Gillian and Catherine were wearing matching oyster dresses and each carrying a single red rose. Gillian's red hair, helped back to its original shade by an upmarket hairdresser in Brighton, had been cut and shaped in curls to just below her shoulders. Both women looked at their very best.

At the end of the ceremony the congregation clapped, and a keyboard player accompanied the flautist in a rendition of 'The Wind Beneath My Wings', while the couple signed the book. Simon gripped Louise's hand.

The wedding breakfast consisted of a lavish five-course meal served at tables by white-gloved waiters. They were seated in a beautifully appointed private dining room with more chandeliers hanging from high ceilings. Handwritten name cards in italic script ensured that Louise and Michelle were seated apart. After the meal, both Catherine and Gillian made a short speech. They described each other with fondness and thanked those people who had supported them over the years. Gillian mentioned Louise as her oldest friend and embarrassed both Louise and Simon, by saying she hoped their wedding would be next. Louise looked away from Michelle.

Louise and Simon chatted in the car on their journey home.

"Well that was some 'do'."

Simon broached the subject of a wedding, "Is it the sort of occasion you would want if we ever married?"

Louise took a deep breath, "Not really, Simon, unless you would like it. It must have cost a fortune, and it's not as if it would be the first time for either of us. I think I'd rather have a quiet, low key, celebration and a decent holiday."

Simon grinned, "Well that's a relief!"

Louise continued the conversation, "If we ever do decide to marry, and we really don't have to unless you want to, then I'd like to enjoy it. I don't want to be bogged down by a thousand arrangements. The other thing is, I am so weary with planning the move and everything else which has happened. I don't think I could cope with arranging anything else at the moment. I just want to enjoy living in our new home together."

They sat in silence for several miles before Louise spoke again, "Tell me what you are thinking, Simon."

"I'm thinking that you are right. We are both knackered, and we still have the visit to the convent to arrange. But, at the same time, I would like to marry you, to make us 'official'."

Louise tried to say something positive.

"Funnily enough, the one thing I really want is to take your name, to be known as 'Mrs Ellis.'"

The thought pleased Simon, "You could do that now, if you wished, take my name."

"That would feel like cheating."

They arrived back in Battle. Each a little dissatisfied with the conversation. They changed out of their wedding clothes, and sat eating toast and drinking coffee. Simon was hesitant, "Lou, there's something I want to ask you. You remember when I got cross because you lied about the counselling?"

"I'll never forget it."

"It was really because I felt cheated on in my marriage to Julie. I guess I am a bit insecure in that respect. Our marriage can wait, it needs to wait, but I would like to do something to make us 'official'. I want to buy you a ring, an engagement ring. You could wear it as confirmation of a promise, your promise that you will marry me and become Mrs Ellis as soon as you feel able." He looked at her, "You're going to cry again, aren't you? I can feel it coming on. Every time I get loving or romantic, you cry." The words were spoken with affection.

"I'm sorry," she sobbed as the tears appeared once more. Simon pulled a tissue from his pocket. "I should have shares in these, you get through so many."

"I can't help it. You make me so happy."

"Can I take that as a yes, then, about the ring?"

"Yes."

"We'll do it next week, before you change your mind. Maybe go to Rye? Unless you would prefer me to use the shopping channel?"

Louise laughed through her sobs.

The matter was settled.

The Final Chapter

It is April 2018, some sixteen months after Louise first discovered that she was adopted. Both the studio and Simon's house in Battle are sold, and Louise and Simon have finally purchased a new home together. It is a converted oast house a few miles from Westfield, East Sussex, the village where Simon lived as a boy. There is a spiral staircase in the living room, which leads to an open plan mezzanine area with far reaching views over the Sussex countryside and the sea beyond. Louise uses the space to paint, but still feels part of the family home. Nana's painting of the grandmother and child is on the wall.

Simon and Louise have further discussed the possibility of marriage, but neither of them feels sufficiently energetic yet to make the arrangements. Louise is now wearing an antique diamond cluster engagement ring set in white gold. It is a classical design. Joan would have approved.

Louise and Simon are travelling in Simon's Mercedes and have reached the outskirts of Chatham. It is their first trip to Kent since the move.

Spring has taken hold of the weather, and Simon and Louise feel the heat of the rays through the car windows. They arrive in Chatham in bright sunshine. Simon notices a judder in the gearbox of his Mercedes, as he turns towards the entrance of the convent.

'I really must persuade Louise that buying myself a new expensive car would be a good investment,' he thinks to himself, 'But maybe not today.'

Louise gets out of the car and rings the bell on the tall cast iron gates. The gates open automatically. Simon notices a camera above the gate post.

"Not short of money, the Catholic Church," he remarks to Louise, trying to ease the tension. A young nun in a mid-blue outfit, wearing a matching headscarf directs them to a parking space.

"Mr Ellis, Mrs Watson, welcome to the Sisters of Mercy. I am Sister Charlotte. I'm sorry about the heavy gates. We are supposed to be an open community, but the Bishop insisted on some extra security after the latest threat. I'm going to take you to see the graves straight away, as that is the main purpose of your visit."

She speaks with a slight northern accent. Both Simon and Louise are surprised and feel guilty at their bias. They had somehow assumed that all nuns were Irish.

"Over the past twenty years, things have changed a lot," explains Sister Charlotte. "We try to reach out to the community with love and forgiveness. We have done our best to show recompense for our past lack of compassion. For example, we've made great efforts to create a tranquil place of rest. We have planted bulbs, and replaced the sign which said 'Illegitimates' with something more sympathetic. We did think about rewriting the gravestones, but they are part of the deceased's history, so we decided to leave them unchanged. I hope you like what we have done. I see you have brought some daffodils with you. We will find an outdoor vase to stand between the graves. They will last longer that way.

Sister Charlotte leads them along a wooded path to a clearing at the back of the convent. It is full of creamy narcissus and purple crocus. Louise holds back the tears. The little wooden sign at the side of the graveyard says 'Mothers and Babies. Loved by our Father in Heaven'.

A tear escapes onto Louise's cheek. Simon grips her hand.

Sister Charlotte points to Patricia's grave, "Your mother is resting there, with her mother next to her."

Sister Charlotte crosses herself and steps backwards. Louise bends down and reads the words which are engraved on each gravestone. One says 'Catherine Makepiece', and on the small headstone beside it are engraved the words 'Patricia Makepiece'. The stones have obviously been cleaned of moss and lichen prior to their visit. Simon's eyes feel tearful, and he pinches himself hard. Louise moves to the back of Patricia's stone and sees the kiss which Ruby secretly carved over sixty-two years ago.

"I must take a photo to show Ruby's daughter. Ruby would have been so pleased that the kiss is still here."

"Are you alright, Louise?" Simon just manages to hold back his own watery emotion, and watches the unstoppable tears stream down Louise's face. He hands her yet another tissue.

"I'm fine. I am not crying with sadness, just pure emotion. She was only fifteen, Simon. What a terrible way to end a young life". A second nun brings a heavy pottery vase full of liquid from the direction of the convent. Louise carefully places the daffodils in the vase, and takes another photo. "I think it's time to go now. I can only manage so much crying in one day."

"You can return any time you wish," says Sister Charlotte.

As they walk towards the car, Simon puts his arm around Louise. "You were so brave. This must be the most important moment of your life."

"Actually, Simon, meeting you was the most important moment of my life, but this comes a very close second."